Where Beautiful Inks

Love is Pain

2

A Poetic Anthology

Edited by:
Brandy Lane

Fort Wayne, Indiana

© 2025 Love is Pain 2; A Poetic Anthology
Editor: Brandy Lane
Foreword: Stevie Flood

Contributing Authors:
D.M. Takeshi, Martin Byrne, Aren Esperanza Goodwin, Gina Carrillo,
Gary S. Watkins, S.D. Kilmer, Joshua Robinson, Blue Carrisole,
Valerie Lorraine, Michelle Chermaine Ramos, Diane Lipton Gollub,
Elizabeth O. Ogunmodede, Caroline Derbes, Kheneil Black, Daphne
Lane, George Oberg, Jimmy Broccoli, Julie Ann Keleher,
Anila Bukhari, Brandy Lane

Published in the United States of America by:
Where Beautiful Inks LLC
Fort Wayne, Indiana

ISBN: 978-1-970359-90-9
Library of Congress Control Number:
2025922081

All pictures throughout this book are available through
Canva and Canva Pro.

DEDICATION

In memory of S.D. Kilmer, who was a dear poet friend of mine. Some of his pieces are lovingly placed in these pages, so that he can live on through his words. Rest in peace, my friend.

To all of those who have loved and lost, but continue to love the lost.

TABLE OF CONTENTS

Martin Byrne *continued*

Aren Esperanza Goodwin

Gina Carrillo

Valerie Lorraine

Valerie Lorraine *continued*

Gary S. Watkins

S.D. Kilmer

Joshua Robinson

George Oberg

Caroline Derbes

Kheneil Black

Kheneil Black *continued*

Elizabeth O. Ogunmodede

Daphne Lane

Diane Lipton Gollub

Jimmy Broccoli

Blue Carrisole

Julie Ann Keleher

Brandy Lane

Brandy Lane *continued*

Where Beautiful Inks

Love is Pain
2

A poetic anthology

FOREWORD

Welcome, dear reader, to the threshold of emotion, where love and pain intertwine like vines in an enchanted garden. Within the confines of these pages lies an odyssey—a journey through the labyrinth of human experience, guided by the words of poets who have dared to confront the complex tapestry of love. In this anthology, aptly titled "Love is Pain," we embark on a voyage of discovery—a pilgrimage through the valleys of ecstasy and the peaks of despair. For love, as these poets remind us, is not merely a fleeting emotion but a force of nature, capable of stirring the deepest recesses of our souls. Through verse and rhyme, meter and prose, these poets weave tales of passion and longing, heartache and redemption. They lay bare their vulnerabilities, inviting us to bear witness to the raw, unfiltered essence of the human condition. As you immerse yourself in these pages, prepare to be captivated by the sheer breadth and depth of emotion on display. For here, amidst the cacophony of voices, you will find solace in the shared experience of love's triumphs and tribulations. So, dear reader, take a deep breath, steel your heart against the inevitable tide of emotion, and surrender yourself to the transformative power of "Love is Pain." For within these words lies the essence of what it means to be human—to love fiercely, to hurt deeply, and to emerge, battered but unbroken, on the other side.

Stevie Flood

*Edited for grammatical errors. Some capitalizations and punctuation preferences are left for artistic effect at the request of the individual authors.

Also, slight variations in local word use and spellings appear, depending on where the poet resides. American English slightly varies from British English.

About
the
Author

DMTakeshi

An extremely disturbed author, DMTakeshi has zero credentials, and these poems have a high probability that they are the ramblings of a person with a serious mental illness. Enjoy!

DMTakeshi, a poetic soul since the tender age of 7, drew inspiration from her beautiful poetess mother. Her poetic journey began with a poignant ode to her grandfather, whom she lost at the age of two. The world only glimpsed her verses in 2021 with the unveiling of her first book, *Unreadable*. Though her initial poetry was tinged with darkness, DMTakeshi, driven by personal growth, shifted her focus to illuminate inspiring narratives, championing happiness and self-love. Here's to her commitment to mental health, spreading joy, and crafting verses that resonate with the brighter facets of life.

Her newest book, *Readable* with *Unreadable* attached, is now available everywhere books are sold!

Find her on Instagram: @DMTakeshi

Defenseless Children
Mother of Us
Loving Me Is New
Missing My Son Haikus
Poetic Life
My Bleeding Heart
Prick
Rooted in My Soul
Sweet Nectar of Lies
Too Hard to Ignore
Especially Kind K
Happiness Effect
DMTakeshi

DMTakeshi

Defenseless Children

You should be in prison
for the physical abuse you put us through.
Even now, you should be locked up—
for you, haven't changed.

You've just grown older,
and without children.
All the lies you made us tell the hospital...
and mom.
You were supposed to be our dad—
someone we could trust.
But it wasn't as such.

You told us not to tell.
You said to say we fell
or that the dresser fell on my chest—
when it was really 280 lbs. of man
jumping on a child.
I could've died!

We had no one to turn to.
Everyone had suspicions,
but never fully knew.
Maybe they would have told.
Maybe they wouldn't.
My mom certainly didn't.

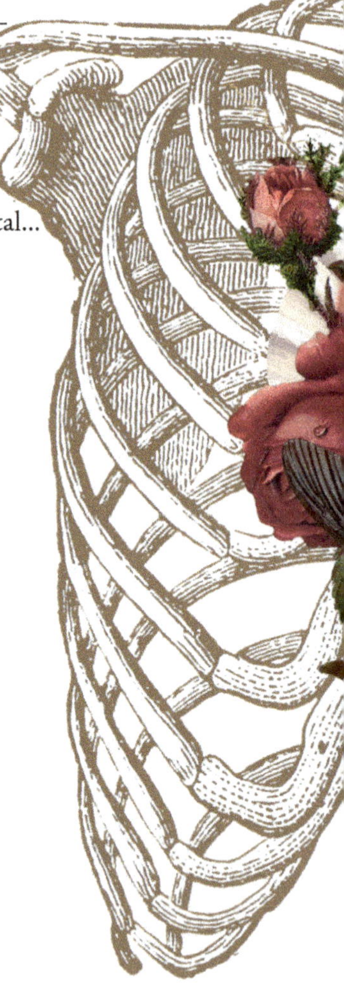

You predators say how it wasn't your fault.
You gaslight and say how much you love us
while streams of fake cries fall from your eyes.
You swear it'll never happen again,
but please, don't let me forget to forgive you.

But then, there is the next time,
and the next, and the next.
Stitches, broken arms, it didn't matter...
It's just to name a few of your many crimes.

But after mom finally left,
you played real nice to win her back,
just like you always did...
But this time it didn't work.

Of course, you blamed it on me
and my bad attitude.
Said I ruined your already failed marriage.
That I ripped off its last appendage.

I was a child.
You were the grown-up.
Your theory—far-fetched and wild.
Maybe she was just tired of your stories—
I don't know why she finally left.
All I know is it was for the best.

W.M. Takeshi

DM Takeshi

Mother of Us

I was a mother of four at age eight.
My three siblings, plus myself.
My parents weren't there.
Mother worked long into the night.
Step-dad, always flying high.
I cared for my children
the best I knew how.

But that's the point;
I didn't know how.
I was furious
and took it out on them.
I wonder where I learned that from…

Doesn't matter.

Point is,
they didn't deserve
to have even more stress back then.
I wasn't the best mother
but I was all they had.

Once I grew,
I tried to be a better role model.
I tried to show them more compassion and love—
because I didn't back then.
The situation wasn't right
for any child to thrive.

They are all grown now,
and have their own children.
I have no concern
that they will not do their best.
Not like I did—I was just a kid.

♡ W.M. Takeshi

Looking right at you, friend.
How beautiful
you are from this view—
very suitable.

I love your eyes, friend,
because they are kind
and your heart extends
beyond most the minds.

Hey friend, I like you!
You're patient people.
My love for you—renewing,
and my mind—growing peaceful.

You are very strong;
today, you stand tall.
You always belong—
giving it your all.

I love you and me.
Me loves I, and you.
Forever to be.
Loving me is new.

Love from head to toes,
a loving spree—
my love for me grows
like a sturdy tree.

Hey you there, stranger,
you have a cool smile—
do me a favor,
know that you're worthwhile.

 *D.M. Takeshi*

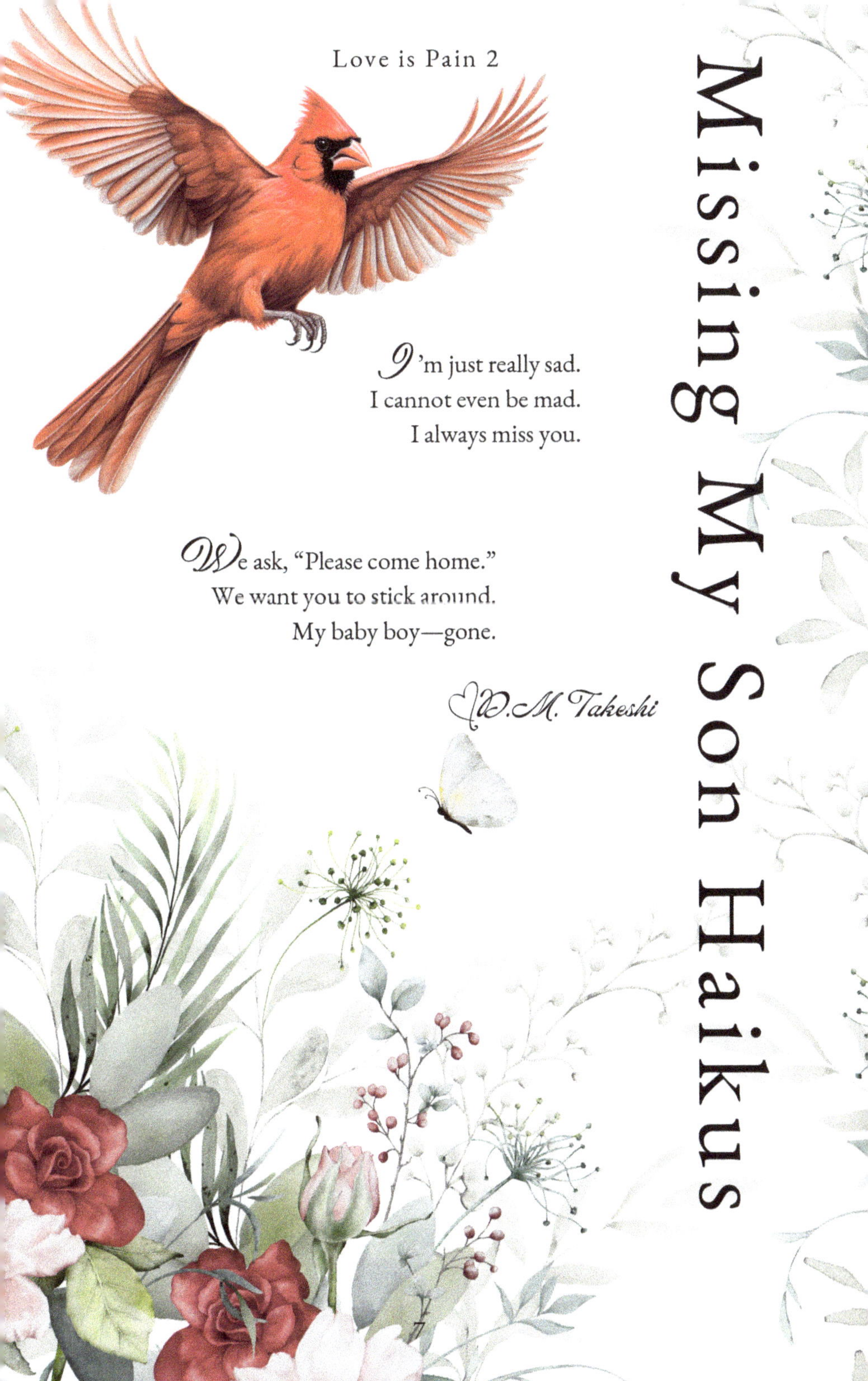

$\mathcal{I}$'m just really sad.
I cannot even be mad.
I always miss you.

$\mathcal{W}$e ask, "Please come home."
We want you to stick around.
My baby boy—gone.

♡ *D.M. Takeshi*

Missing My Son Haikus

DM Takeshi

As I pen my thoughts,
or computer my words,
I feel like a fraud,
and my brain just hurts

Poetic skeptic
unsure of my prose,
majestic, pathetic,
hit right on the nose.

My self-worth is hurt every time
that I only get a few likes—
more cool to be the paradigm
instead of going through these strikes.

Self-doubt hasn't really served me,
yet I eat the entire pie.
My very next guarantee...
a poet struggles to get by.

No confidence after all this time...
It really *CAN'T* be *THAT* hard to rhyme.

D.M. Takeshi

Poetic Life

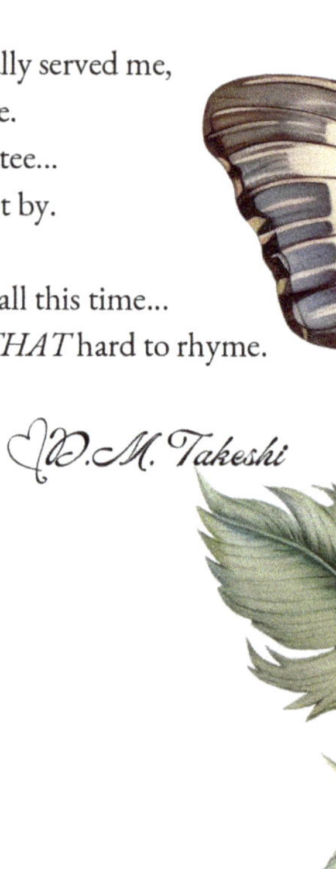

My Bleeding Heart

I failed and didn't show up
when I was supposed to.
Did it hurt you too,
or did you even notice?
Maybe for you it was a bonus.

You're nervous to see me
like I'm some kind of monster,
if only you could see
the love I have to offer.

I hope one day you'll remember
all the great times we had together.

♡ *W.M. Takeshi*

DM Takeshi

Let me tell you about a boy named Nick;
a young girl fell in love,
even though it was a trick.

A hurricane of emotions came.
When she quickly became pregnant
she was put to shame
for wanting to keep her baby.

Shoving turned to punches
and this was the end of them—
but then began the grudges,
and the threats began.

A whole year of checking over my shoulder
afraid of what you said would happen.
You turned ugly, bolder,
I needed to take action.

I finally stood up for myself and my son,
I couldn't let you threaten our lives anymore!
I was finally done.
I'd never let you see us again, I swore.

Now my son has chosen to live with him.
Prick wins.

D.M. Takeshi

Prick

My son sent me a hateful message.
My life was in wreckage,
for my fear kicked in
that I was losing him.

Today, he apologized.
I was indeed surprised.
I wanted to immediately forgive,
for we only have one life to live.

Plus, I have a deep love for him
rooted in my soul,
even though lately it has been
seriously out of control.

I worry dearly about his mental health,
unlike any anxieties I have ever felt.
My hope for him is to heal,
for his hurt is very real.

If he ever reads this,
I want him to always know
how very special he is.
I hope he understands it when feeling low.

My son is rooted deep in my soul,
his love makes me feel so very whole.

Rooted In My Soul

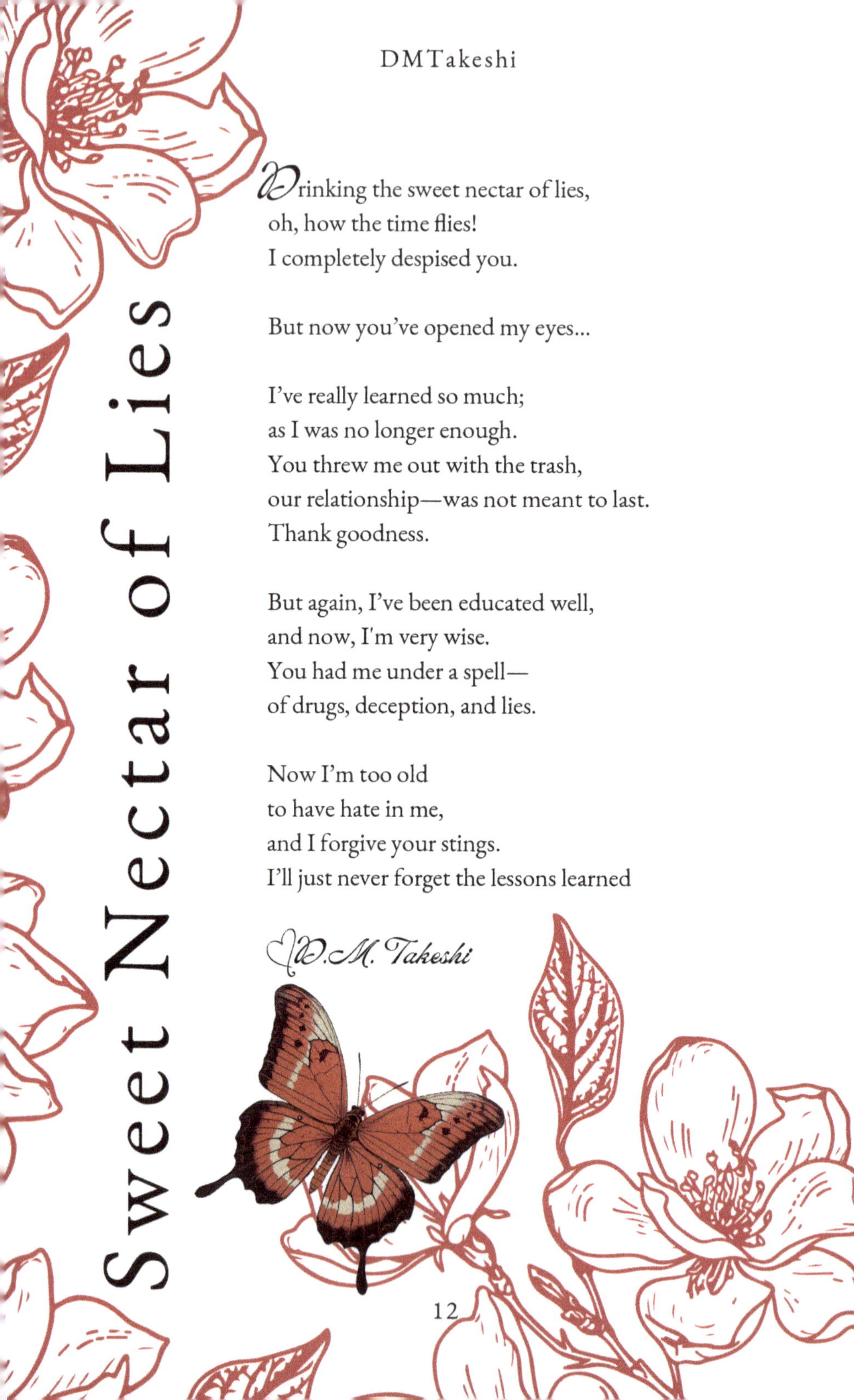

Sweet Nectar of Lies

Drinking the sweet nectar of lies,
oh, how the time flies!
I completely despised you.

But now you've opened my eyes...

I've really learned so much;
as I was no longer enough.
You threw me out with the trash,
our relationship—was not meant to last.
Thank goodness.

But again, I've been educated well,
and now, I'm very wise.
You had me under a spell—
of drugs, deception, and lies.

Now I'm too old
to have hate in me,
and I forgive your stings.
I'll just never forget the lessons learned

D.M. Takeshi

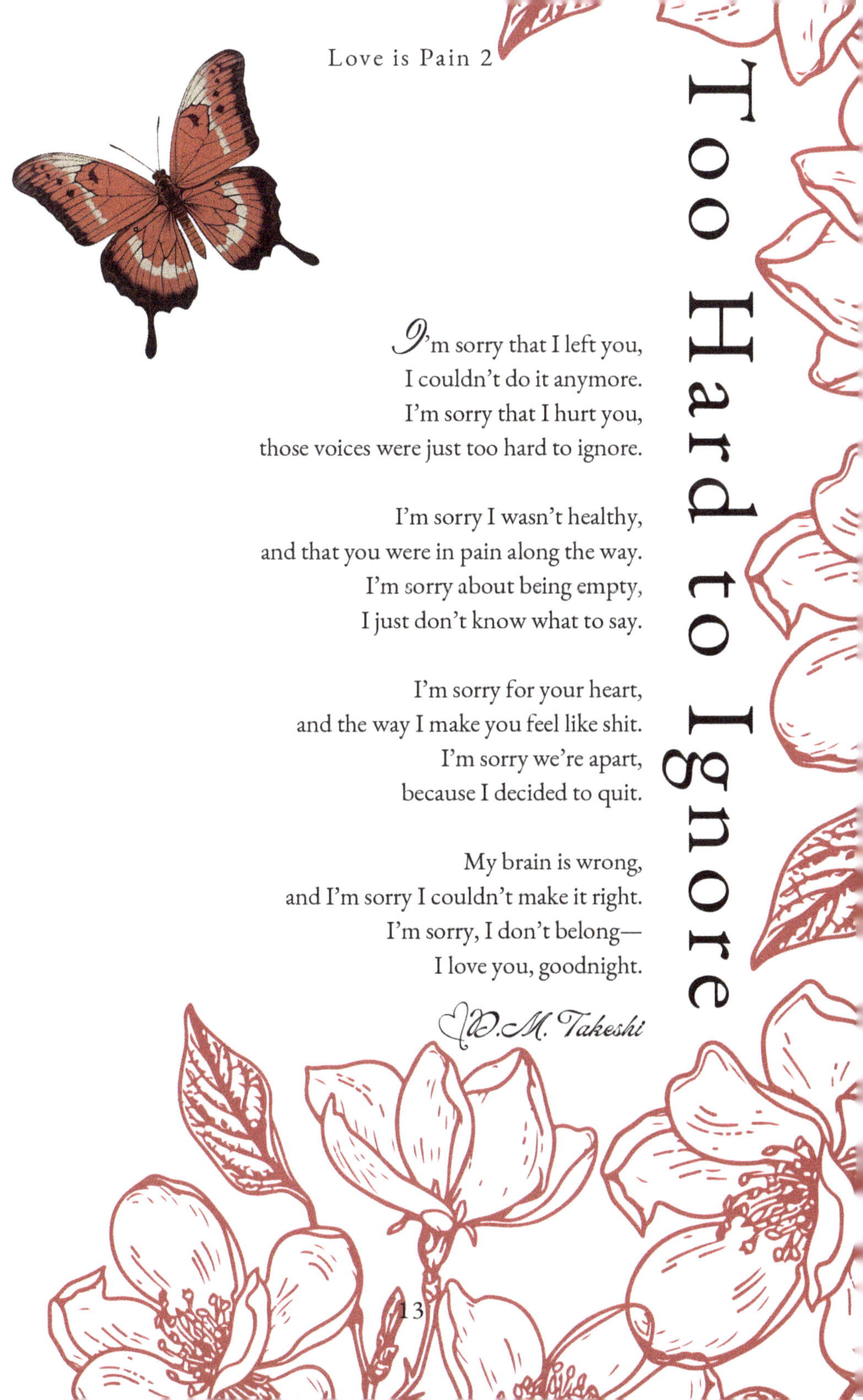

Too Hard to Ignore

I'm sorry that I left you,
I couldn't do it anymore.
I'm sorry that I hurt you,
those voices were just too hard to ignore.

I'm sorry I wasn't healthy,
and that you were in pain along the way.
I'm sorry about being empty,
I just don't know what to say.

I'm sorry for your heart,
and the way I make you feel like shit.
I'm sorry we're apart,
because I decided to quit.

My brain is wrong,
and I'm sorry I couldn't make it right.
I'm sorry, I don't belong—
I love you, goodnight.

D. M. Takeshi

DM Takeshi

I've never really felt this way,
you make me want to scream—
especially because you're kind,
oKay, but that's not your whole scheme.

You take me for a ride
and I love it,
down the mental slide,
I'll tough it.

Baby, just take me away.
Let me feel my wings.
Especially kind k.
Lessons from the kings.

You've left me in a whirl,
now I know my purpose.
Something about this crazy world
left me with mighty urges.

This I want to convey,
I'm bursting at the seams;
especially kind k,
mother of the queens.

D. M. Takeshi

*I*n the midst of all this potency,
I'd like to be read like a book, openly.
I'd like to share with you my poetry,
so that one day, I'll inspire you—hopefully.

I'm on my journey to inspire the masses.
To reach for the stars through happiness.
I'm gonna make sure to take all the chances.
This life provides to ensure to advance us.

I'm tired of making excuses,
it's only left scars and bruises;
most times she misuses—
it's only meant to confuse us.

It's time to for me to spread my influence;
one thing at a time on which to focus.
Good judgement commingled with prudence,
lead with my heart for the hopeless to notice.

This is ultimately for me—
fantasy turned reality.
It's also about family...

In all actuality,
happiness is where I'd rather be.

D.M. Takeshi

About the Author

Martin Byrne

Martin Byrne was born and raised in Liverpool, England. Graduating from school, he embarked on many and varied careers, including mechanical engineering, hospitality, and transportation. His love of reading adventure stories as a child, also fueled his desire to travel. Currently resident in Denmark, he has two boys with his ex-wife. Although writing poetry is a hobby for him, he draws inspiration from his life experiences as well as the beauty of nature that surrounds the small seaside town where he lives.

Magazine publications: one piece in *Unicorn Magazine*, Vol No.6, December 2021.

Anthology: three pieces, one in each volume of *Unchaining Freedom Trilogy* (Our Earthians Community Group), Ink Gladiator Press 2022.

Anthology: six pieces in *Winter: A Poetic Anthology,* Where Beautiful Inks 2023.

Martin Byrne

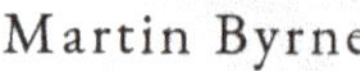

Martin Byrne

I see the kindness in your eyes.
Am I not blessed by your smile?
Can we not embrace the love
you say that does not exist?

When I comforted you
in the fold of my arms,
are the promises made
no longer etched in stone?

I do not understand
when you say you don't feel,
and the silence between us
increases exponentially;
like fallow fall leaves
heralding the change, of
summers' drift to autumn—
or the languid glow
of a golden sun,
pouring like honey
on your soft warm skin.

Always, I'd succumb,
falling slowly and gently
into, the depth of your kiss.

♡ M. Byrne

Surrender

Memories linger like grains of sand

And then the waves crash on the beach,

Resplendent in power and awe, before

Retreating to the murky deep.

I watch the flow and ebb diminish,

Amour passes by, arrows sheathed.

Going to pastures new, it seems

Eternity, is out of reach.

M. Byrne

Decree Absolute

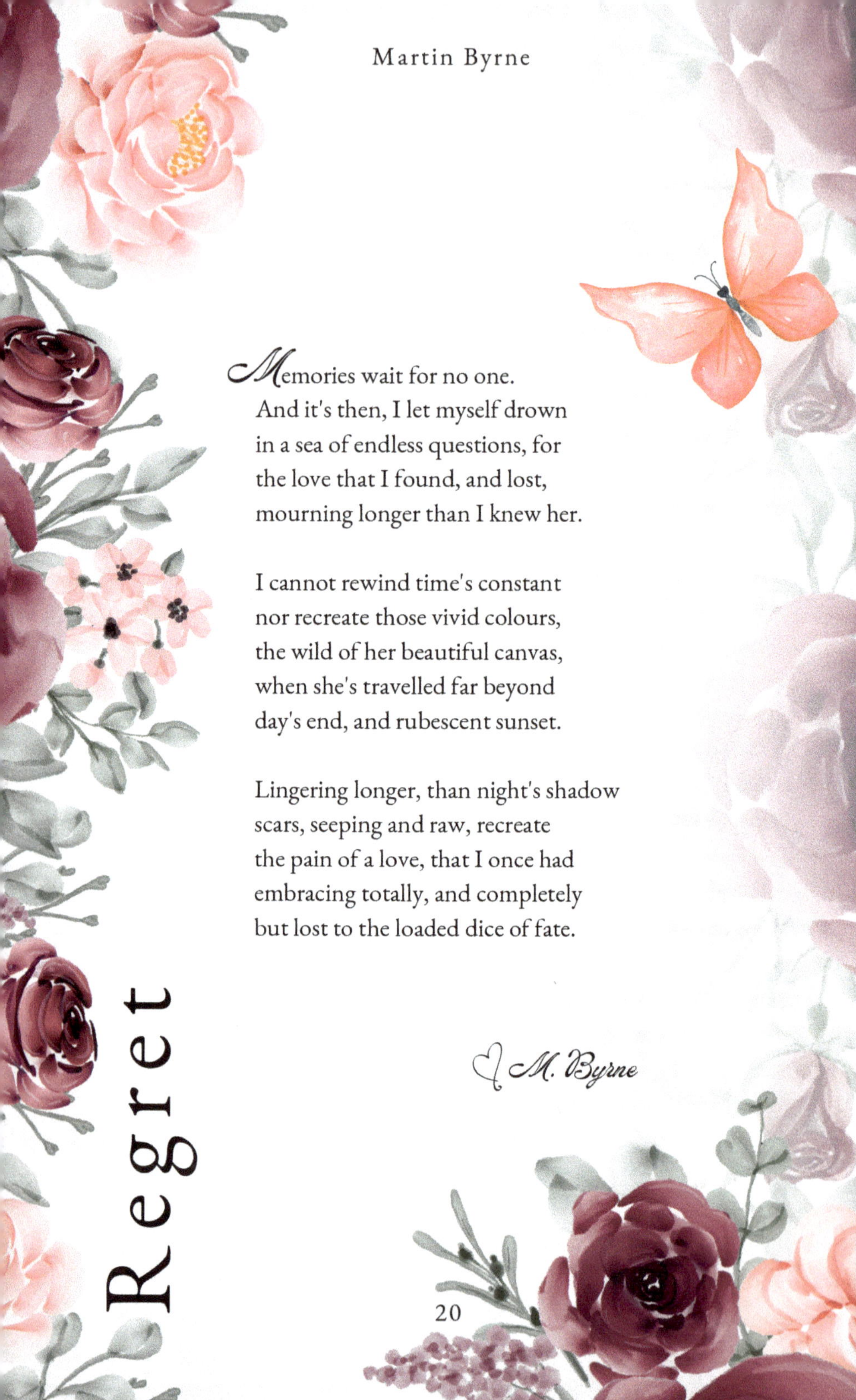

Memories wait for no one.
And it's then, I let myself drown
in a sea of endless questions, for
the love that I found, and lost,
mourning longer than I knew her.

I cannot rewind time's constant
nor recreate those vivid colours,
the wild of her beautiful canvas,
when she's travelled far beyond
day's end, and rubescent sunset.

Lingering longer, than night's shadow
scars, seeping and raw, recreate
the pain of a love, that I once had
embracing totally, and completely
but lost to the loaded dice of fate.

M. Byrne

Did you stop to think, the day before the day?
Did you realise, the heart that you would break?
I thought that it'd never end, the love that we had found.
But at the bus stop on that day, my world would come undone.
With you, who I'd come to love,
and you, who gave me love.
With you, I would touch the stars,
then discarded, on that fateful day—
all those years ago.

In the months that followed, I'd see you in the park.
I'd see you in the market, and in our local bar.
I'd see you in a restaurant, together with my friends.
I'd see you in my dreams at night, would this ever end?
With you, who I'd come to love,
and you, who gave me love.
Then you, made me look the fool
When you lied, on that fateful day—
all those years ago.

I kept some pictures of you, and letters that you wrote.
I kept on hoping beyond hope, that time could be *rewrote*.
I never, ever can forget the warmth of your kiss.
And when I held you close, the pleasure of your touch.
With you, whom I'd come to love,
and you, who gave me love.
Through you, I will always have
the memories of eternal love—
all those years ago.

M. Byrne

Martin Byrne

Did you forget to say goodbye?
Or did you leave on purpose?
Time and place are irrelevant
the void impresses permanence
when I can't recall the laughter
or the sparkle in your eyes.

Feelings linger through a haze
but should there not be something
that is more than just a dream?
Letters of love or photographs—
mementos that you were real?

Though wisdom says the pain will wane,
still I clutch in desperation
to the words that melted my heart.
You said you would always love me!

So why can I not comprehend
the reason that you left—
or why you could not tell me?

All at Sea

Letting Go

Silence reverberates in the empty room
echoing off the walls, back to back.
Reasoned thought doesn't explain;
the crushing weight, the pressure
that encompasses an ocean-deep,
the grey between night and day.

Conversations, just out of reach,
another world, another life.
Murmuring words that impeach
the clarity of a mountain lake,
and ripples that disturb
the tranquil peace he yearns.

The veil descends, the cobalt sky;
opaque, vague, and distant fade—
as drowning voices turn silent.
Walls, melting to nothing.
Stars, streaking to a blur.
Infinity, in a pinpoint of light.

Awake in a familiar room,
hazy figures of loved ones' past
embrace the lonely child —
and welcome him back home.

J. M. Byrne

Martin Byrne

Slipped from sight but not from the mind—
an image etched in eternity.
Steady as the night, full of stars,
whose light has travelled endlessly.
Love will never cease or fade
its essence lingers in the heavens.
A beacon of infinite suns
across the universe.
That precious cargo stays
when it is our time to leave.
Don't grieve too long.
We've not gone far.
We're just around the corner,
where we'll wait until you find us.

♡ M. Byrne

Linger

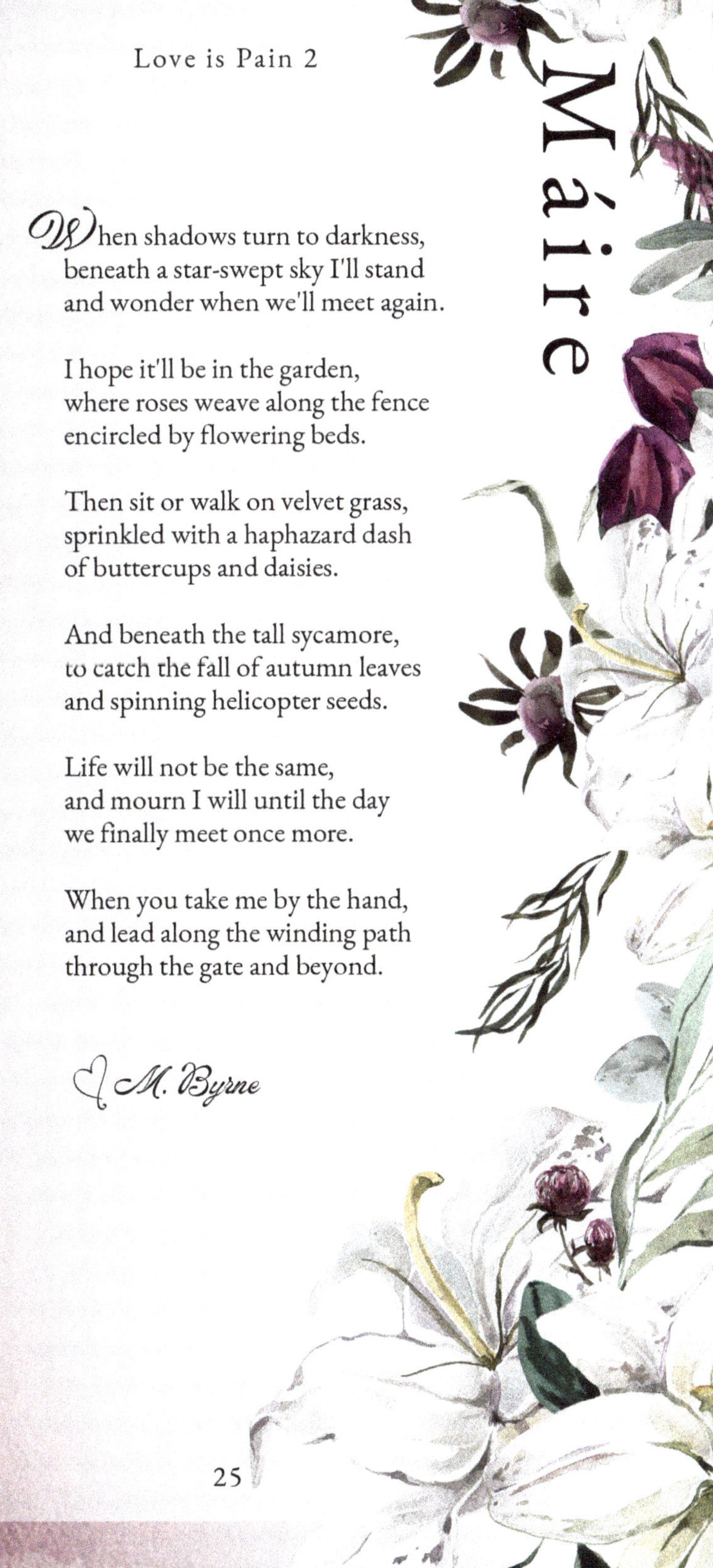

When shadows turn to darkness,
beneath a star-swept sky I'll stand
and wonder when we'll meet again.

I hope it'll be in the garden,
where roses weave along the fence
encircled by flowering beds.

Then sit or walk on velvet grass,
sprinkled with a haphazard dash
of buttercups and daisies.

And beneath the tall sycamore,
to catch the fall of autumn leaves
and spinning helicopter seeds.

Life will not be the same,
and mourn I will until the day
we finally meet once more.

When you take me by the hand,
and lead along the winding path
through the gate and beyond.

♡ M. Byrne

Martin Byrne

Hanging On

The stony path is worn and unkempt
winding under dense, arched branches
as thick air presses like a heavy
blanket, an oppressive stifling heat,
clammy on clothes and skin.
Between the trees, dark shadows lurk
sensing eyes, deathly and cold, watch
while creeping, pervasive fingers
reach out to grasp my soul.

Running into an open clearing
a country house stands small and lonely.
Tended plants and shrubs grow wild, hanging
and lifeless in the scorching sun,
abandoned and forlorn.
Rising memories flood like the tide
stirring emotions, once submerged
and feelings I thought were forgotten
return again to the fore.

It did not feel like aeons had passed
I swam in your sensuous ocean
felt the warm crush of your ruby lips
loving like there was no tomorrow
lost, in Elysium.
Such heavenly bliss, could not last
when the cruel hand of fate, struck
and stole like a thief in the night;
your kiss, your love, your life.

But still I see you, your shadow through
every window and every curtain
footsteps echoing in empty rooms
and your presence lingers like dust
that hangs in a beam of sunlight.
So year on year, compelled to return
I cling on to, the memory of you
like a drowning man, clings on to life
fearing, to let go.

M. Byrne

*L*ook at me standing
here on my own again,
embracing the ghost of you.
Stories inscribed in mirrors
reflections of distant lives.
Pictures from a far-flung reality—
and still, I hold on to
the image of you leaving.

Take my impassioned love,
beyond a place I wish not to know.
When feelings— empty and forgotten,
rise then fall. And still, I want more.

The truth—is hard to hear.
Words—become incomprehensible.
Senses—wanting yet imperceptive to
a language I've yet to understand.

♡ M. Byrne

Doors

Time

What happened to the life I envisioned?
It slipped so easily through open fingers.
Rushing instead from shore to shore;
chasing fantasies like summer breezes,
the tumbling flight of autumn leaves
casting dreams, like shiny flat pebbles that
skim and hop over eddying currents,
and sparkling swirls of stoic streams.
Memories gradually drifting out
to the vast and empty cold sea.

When did they fall, the walls of my castle?
Apparently built on uncertain foundations.
Hourglass turned, I counted grains of sand,
then counted the inclining sweep of the stars;
and counted the seconds, the days, and the years.
Left behind my anchor of life and love—
waiting for time to catch up, I stood still;
watching instead, the setting sun flame
magnificently beyond the horizon.

If time is measured in grains of sand,
do our lives linger, forever in an hourglass?

♡ *M. Byrne*

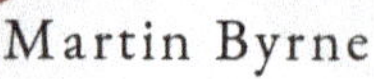

Martin Byrne

The Dance

Tiny lights trace along the wall
gliding circuitous across the floor
from the twinkling star above.
Beauty, sparkling in your eyes
like multifaceted diamonds
shining, brighter than the sun.

Hand in hand, cheek to cheek,
your soft warm skin radiates
a potent and heady fragrance
laced with subtle, delicate notes
of jasmine, citrus, and vanilla.
Senses, infected with your aura,
I sink in your deep ocean.

Like the celestial bodies above,
we're captured by the dance—
spinning gently and effortlessly
through figures, veiled and indistinct;
who part - inconspicuously
like some biblical sea, guiding us
to where we should go.

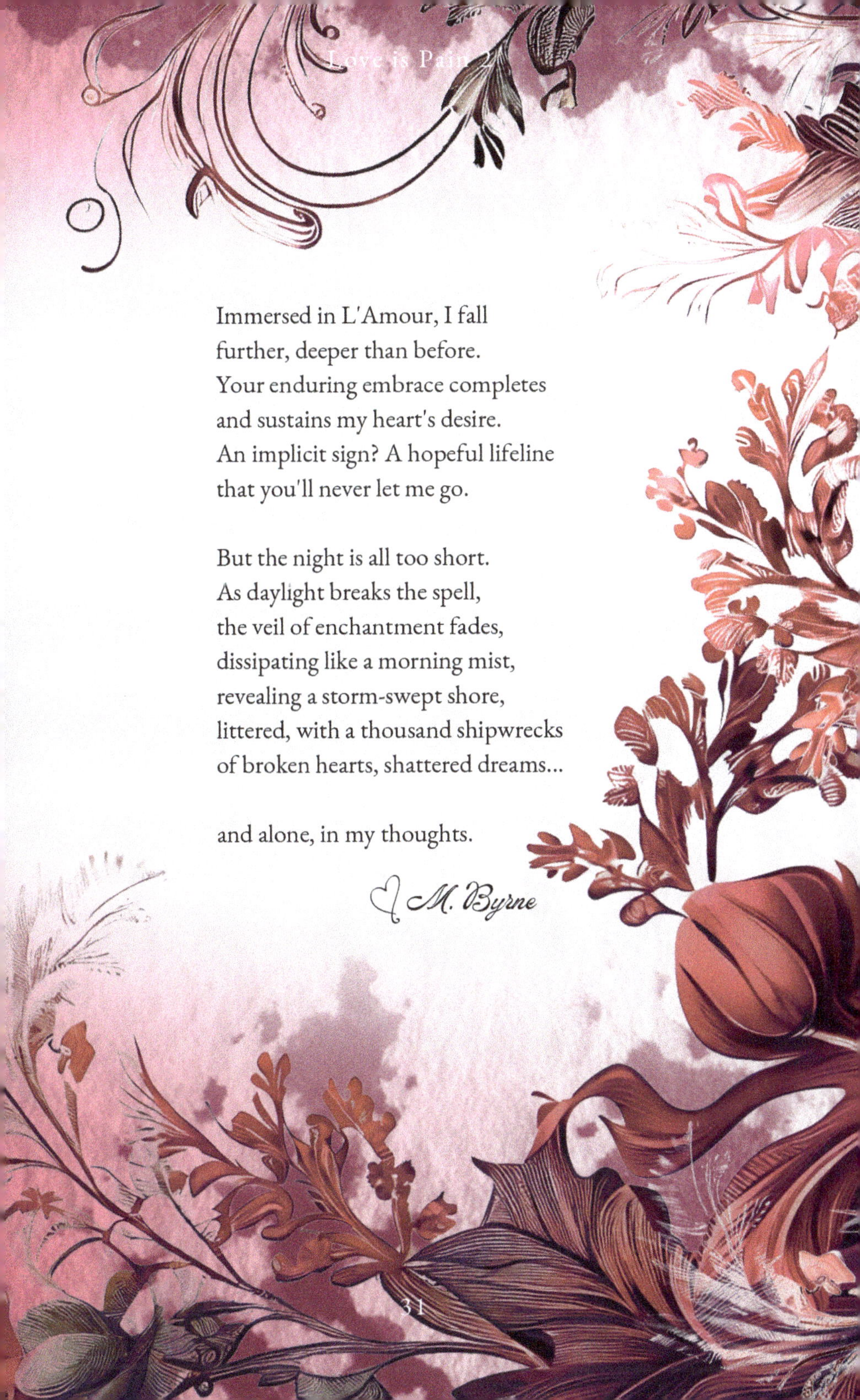

Immersed in L'Amour, I fall
further, deeper than before.
Your enduring embrace completes
and sustains my heart's desire.
An implicit sign? A hopeful lifeline
that you'll never let me go.

But the night is all too short.
As daylight breaks the spell,
the veil of enchantment fades,
dissipating like a morning mist,
revealing a storm-swept shore,
littered, with a thousand shipwrecks
of broken hearts, shattered dreams...

and alone, in my thoughts.

♡ M. Byrne

About the Author

Aren Esperanza Goodwin

Aren Esperanza Goodwin grew up in the Colorado Rocky Mountains. Raised on the lyrics and ideas found in bluegrass music, classic rock, folk, and the ever-echoic Grateful Dead, she nurtured a love for poetry and lyricism at a young age. Finding her voice in the language of poetry gave her the strength and insight to rise out from under a life of normalized abuse, addiction, and gender dysphoria. Through poetry, these struggles were given wings and sculpted into something beautiful. This gave her the freedom to release and love her struggles and the growth they brought, while simultaneously loosening her grip on the pain and fear she harbored in their name. If asked, she would swear time and time again that scribbling rhymes and rhythms on scrap paper during her 15-minute work breaks led to a passion that would prove to be nothing short of life-saving in later years. Now, her motivation lives on through the desire to share her experiences with any soul struggling similarly.

You can find more from Aren here:
https://dimopus.com/

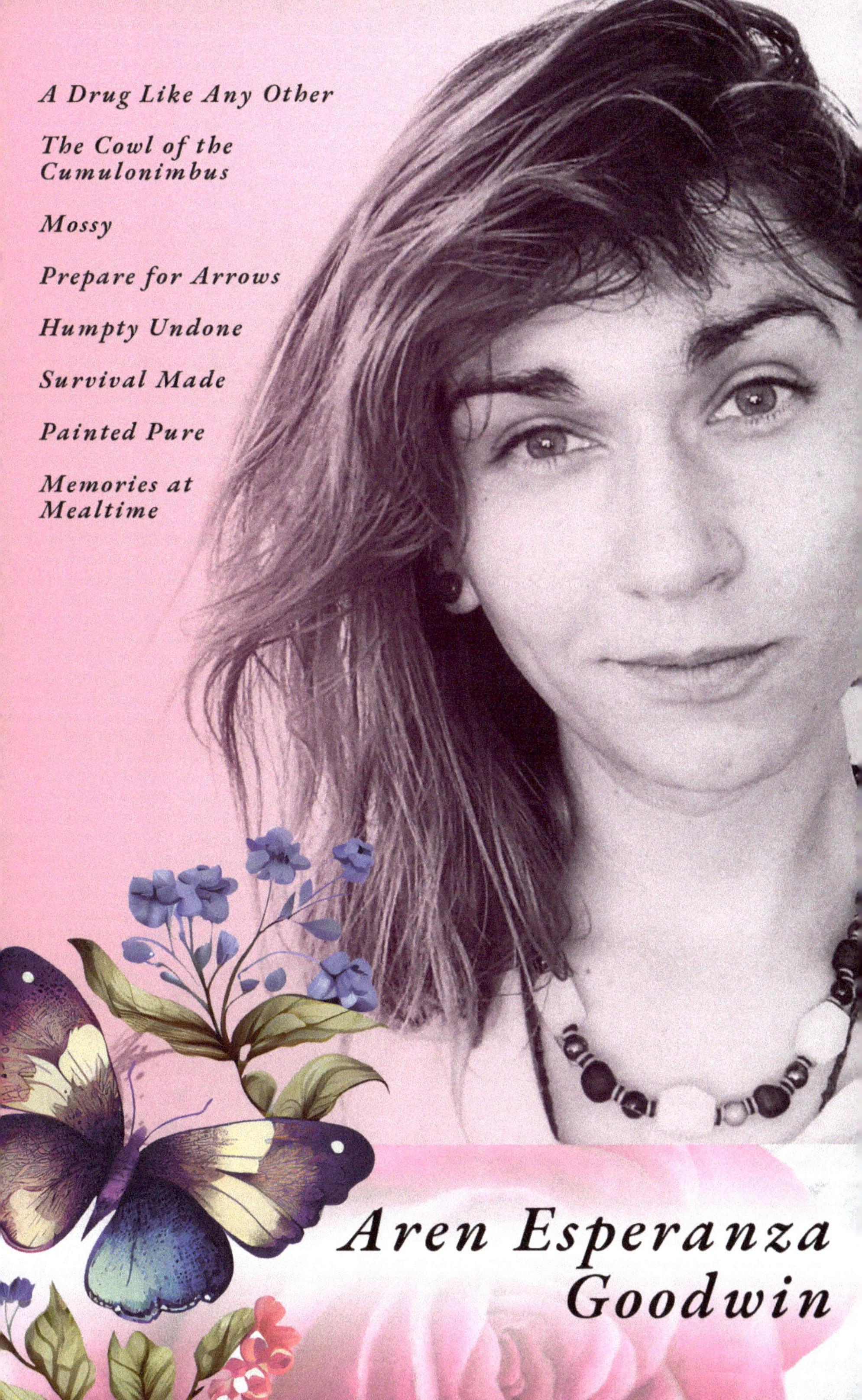

A Drug Like Any Other
The Cowl of the Cumulonimbus
Mossy
Prepare for Arrows
Humpty Undone
Survival Made
Painted Pure
Memories at Mealtime
Aren Esperanza Goodwin

Aren Esperanza Goodwin

A Drug Like Any Other

I remember the days that we spent bent together fondly.
Before the pebble path grew paper-thin,
and the blank lines came to haunt me.
You see, love's a drug like any other,
though served with sympathetic hugs—
of which I've just enough ingested to restore my collapsed lungs.
For consistency, to me,
now means only lost hope and overdose.
As I've seen how sickness seeds in the unplowed overgrowth.
I left the cobbles unconsidered,
feeding fire through my liver.
So now I live to die,
with withered eyes,
for I've no night sky left to give her.

If I could, I'd ease your pain.
And should you ask, I'd end the needless strain.
Live free of games,
and take knee—when you breathe my name.

In every dream, you say the same shit.
Till I awake and further blame,
myself, my fear,
and empty ears,
for the coming cutthroat years.

My love, I beg you,
let go of my hand.
For fear, I'll disappear damaged again.
   In those moments, she pleaded,
your pain and hatred's too heavy.
I know with that kind of weight,
I could never fly steady.
So I beg you, let go of my legs,
as I disappear, damaged instead.

   On how many hopes have we dined?
Due to our decisionless existence,
won't you make up my mind?
Seems I never find the time.
And when I unwind,
I'm uninclined,
   to straighten my braided spine,
      and take stock of the weighted tines.
         Before the fork finds my mouth,
         and sends another one south.
         By expectations driven out.
         Cuz I can't find the time to talk about,
         my pouting face, you somehow pleased.
         You're the color, cut out till I'm see through.
         So sorry I deceived you.
         It's this cutting kind of cold
         which forms the memories,
         that come along and fucking eat you...

The Cowl of the Cumulonimbus

Aren Esperanza Goodwin

For years I've mulled about upon this mountain,
beside a river bed run dry as I.
It is here I climbed,
to flee the field of prying eyes.
To escape a faulty place,
where the prideful scry you from the side....
But, that's reactive crap!
You see,
as time passed, my mind relaxed.
In fact,
I can't help but miss the healing parts.
Like lips and teeth,
that speak to weakened hearts,
and lead them, fiending, from the dark.

So, as twilight thickens on this mountaintop,
I wish a moving mouth
would make my motor stop.
Skip a spin, or half-heard beat,
just a jolt enough to make me drop.
But here I only hear the thunder.
It appears,
the cowl of the cumulonimbus,
I am far from under.
So lightning never strikes.
No, it never sets my kite alight...
And, in hindsight,
I'd soon trade toiling at this height,
for a patient peck, or playful bite.

♡ÆG

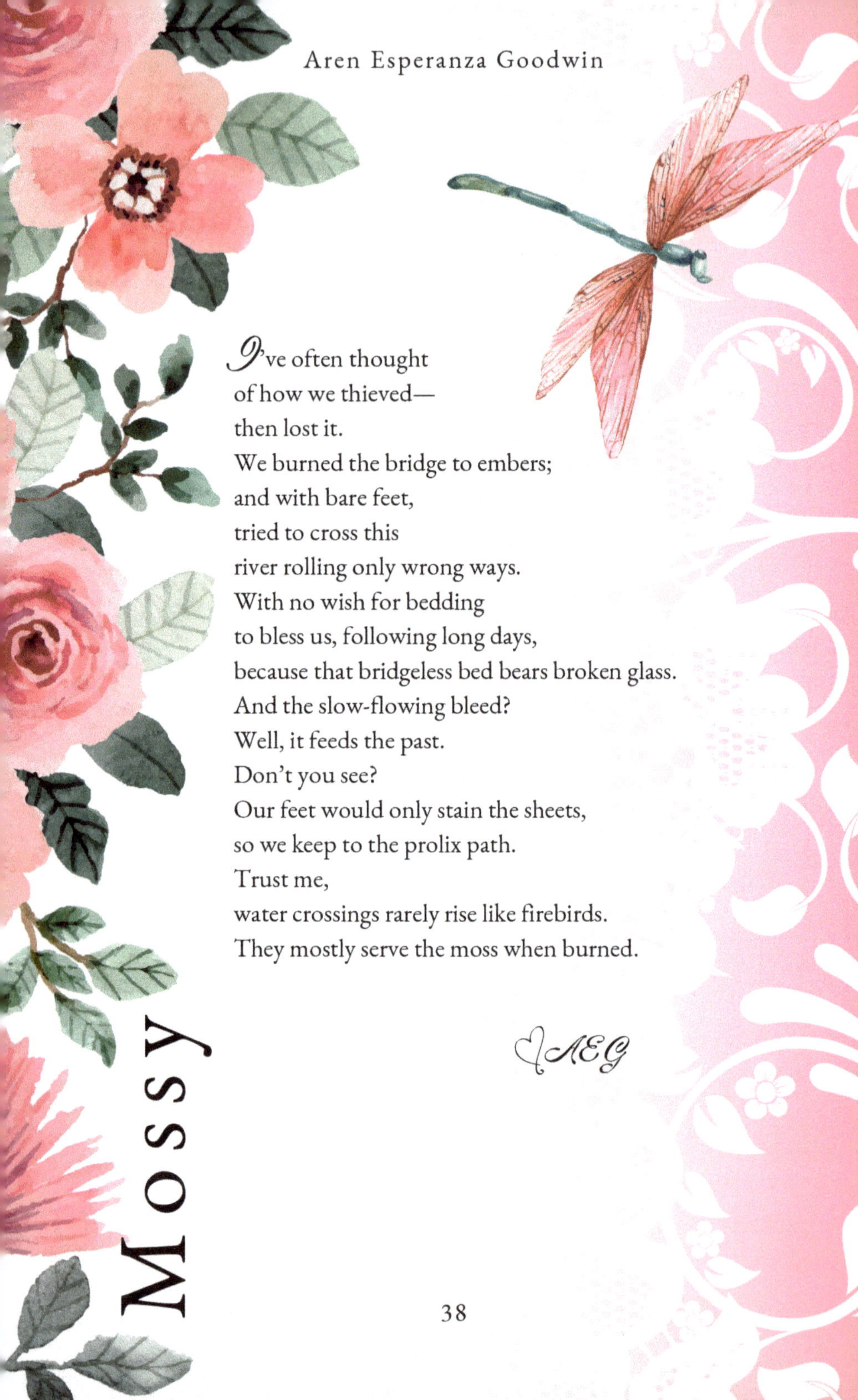

Aren Esperanza Goodwin

I've often thought
of how we thieved—
then lost it.
We burned the bridge to embers;
and with bare feet,
tried to cross this
river rolling only wrong ways.
With no wish for bedding
to bless us, following long days,
because that bridgeless bed bears broken glass.
And the slow-flowing bleed?
Well, it feeds the past.
Don't you see?
Our feet would only stain the sheets,
so we keep to the prolix path.
Trust me,
water crossings rarely rise like firebirds.
They mostly serve the moss when burned.

♡ AEG

Mossy

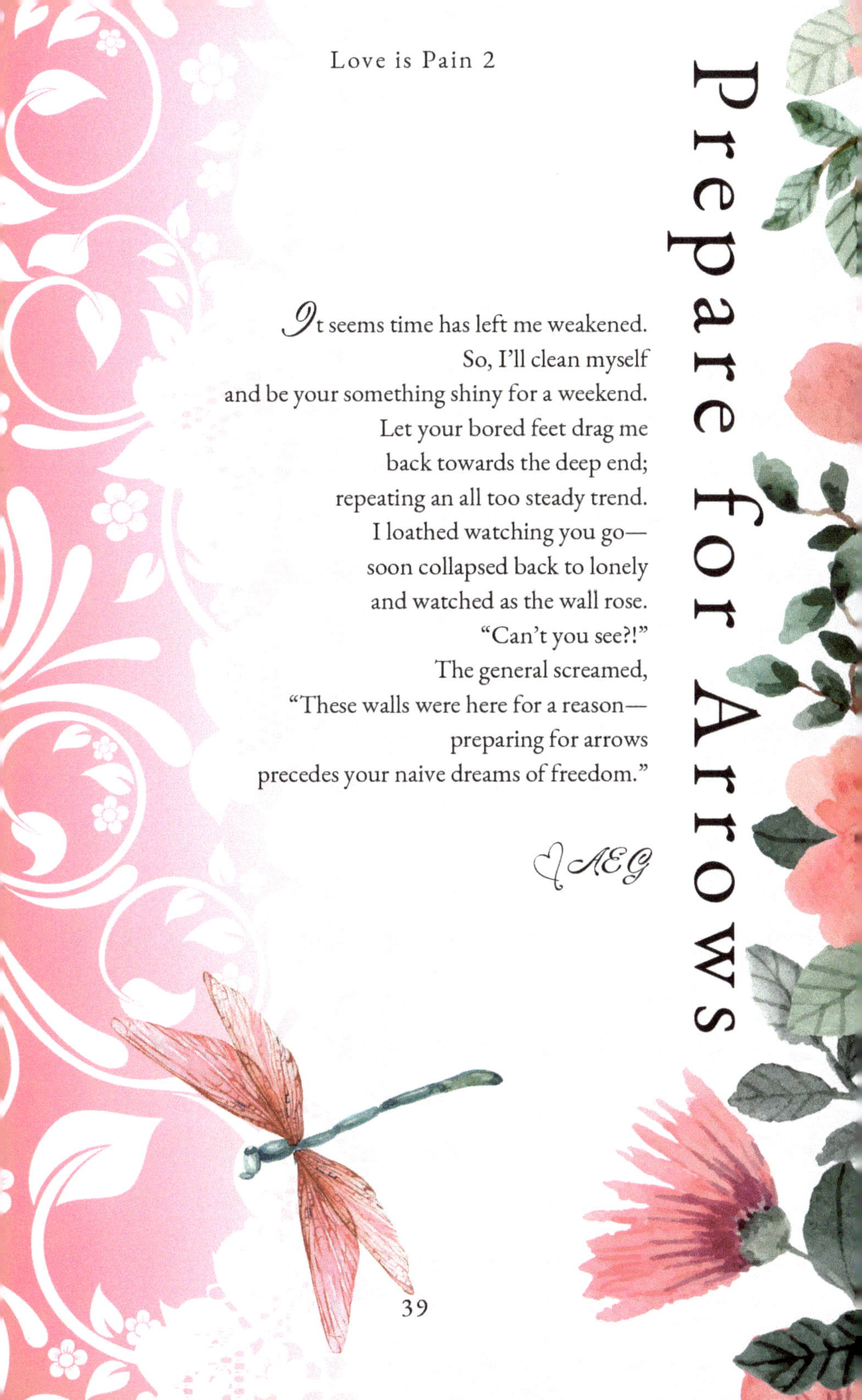

It seems time has left me weakened.
So, I'll clean myself
and be your something shiny for a weekend.
Let your bored feet drag me
back towards the deep end;
repeating an all too steady trend.
I loathed watching you go—
soon collapsed back to lonely
and watched as the wall rose.
"Can't you see?!"
The general screamed,
"These walls were here for a reason—
preparing for arrows
precedes your naive dreams of freedom."

♡ AEG

Prepare for Arrows

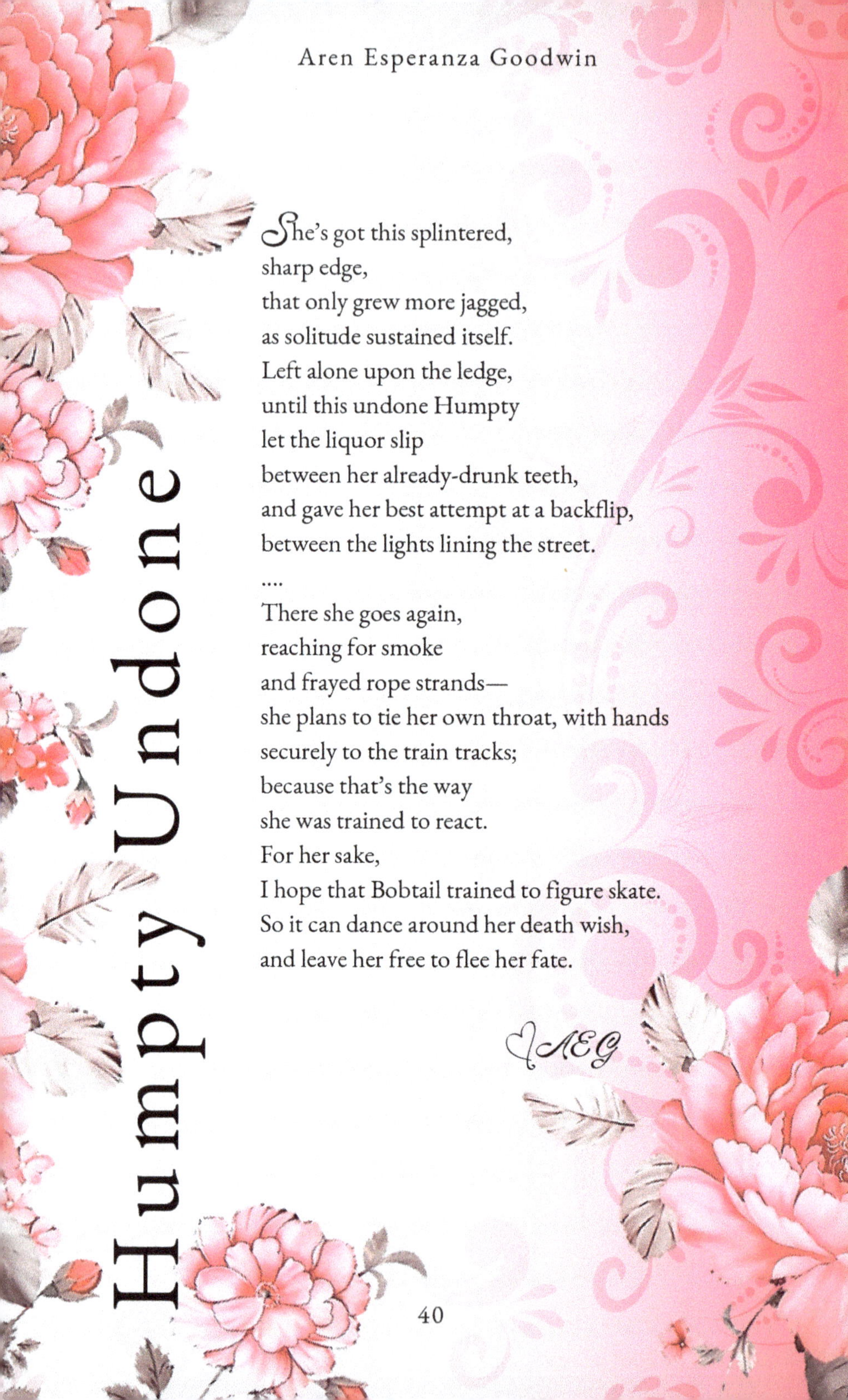

Aren Esperanza Goodwin

Humpty Undone

She's got this splintered,
sharp edge,
that only grew more jagged,
as solitude sustained itself.
Left alone upon the ledge,
until this undone Humpty
let the liquor slip
between her already-drunk teeth,
and gave her best attempt at a backflip,
between the lights lining the street.
....
There she goes again,
reaching for smoke
and frayed rope strands—
she plans to tie her own throat, with hands
securely to the train tracks;
because that's the way
she was trained to react.
For her sake,
I hope that Bobtail trained to figure skate.
So it can dance around her death wish,
and leave her free to flee her fate.

AEG

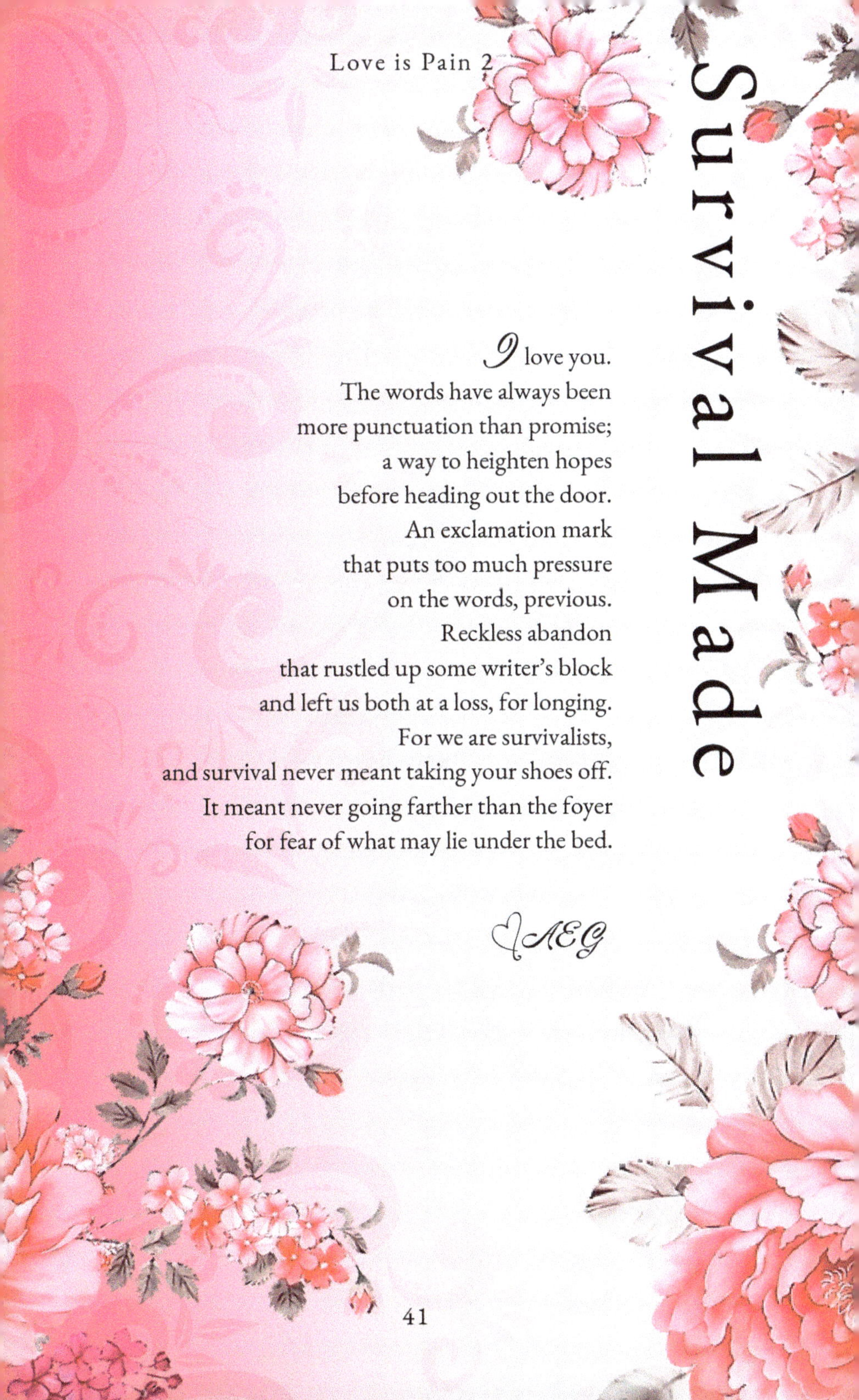

Survival Made

I love you.
The words have always been
more punctuation than promise;
a way to heighten hopes
before heading out the door.
An exclamation mark
that puts too much pressure
on the words, previous.
Reckless abandon
that rustled up some writer's block
and left us both at a loss, for longing.
For we are survivalists,
and survival never meant taking your shoes off.
It meant never going farther than the foyer
for fear of what may lie under the bed.

♡AEG

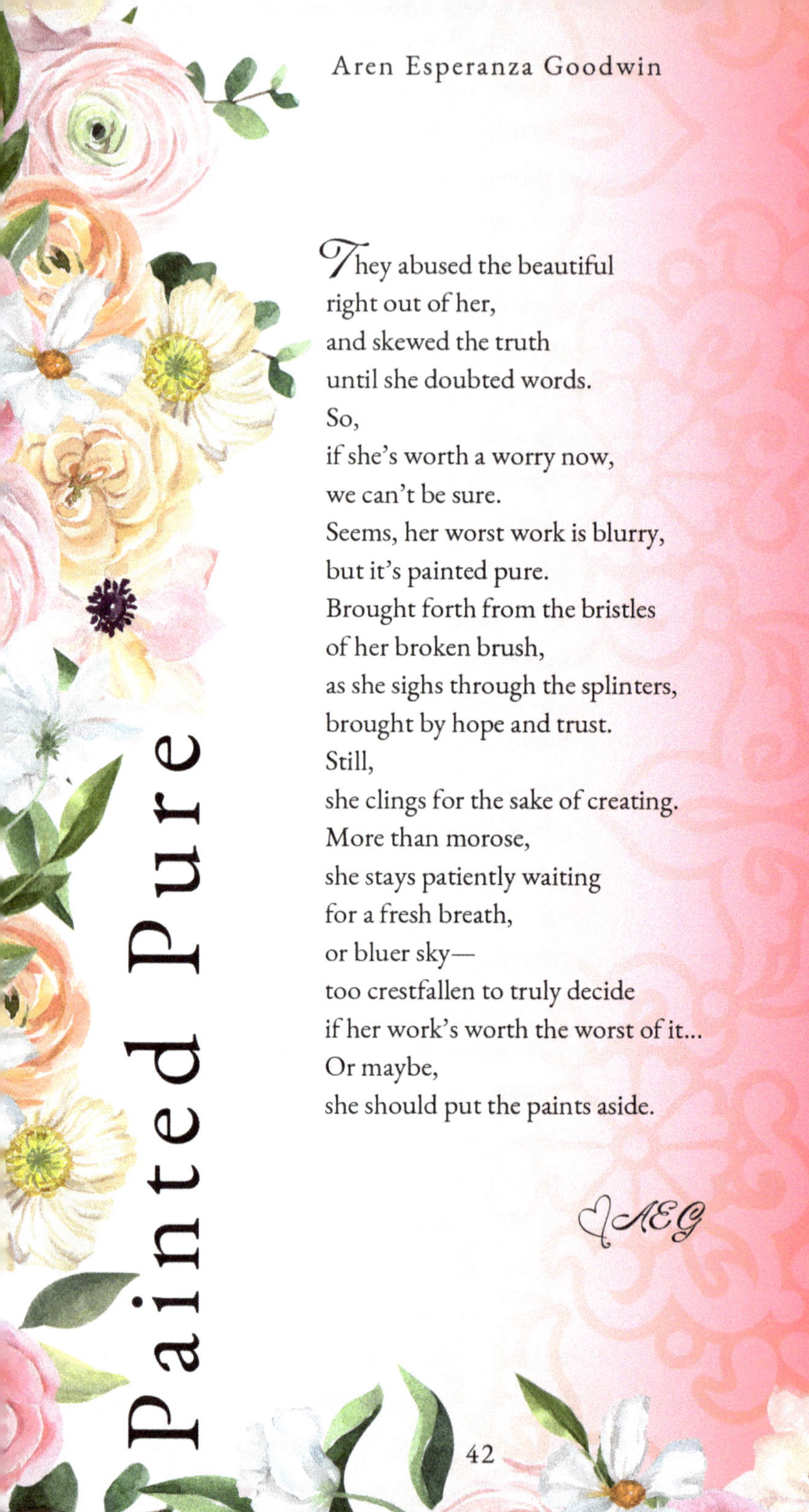

Aren Esperanza Goodwin

Painted Pure

They abused the beautiful
right out of her,
and skewed the truth
until she doubted words.
So,
if she's worth a worry now,
we can't be sure.
Seems, her worst work is blurry,
but it's painted pure.
Brought forth from the bristles
of her broken brush,
as she sighs through the splinters,
brought by hope and trust.
Still,
she clings for the sake of creating.
More than morose,
she stays patiently waiting
for a fresh breath,
or bluer sky—
too crestfallen to truly decide
if her work's worth the worst of it...
Or maybe,
she should put the paints aside.

♡AEG

And so, memories of you gather like feral felines around my feet at the sound of an opening can or the crack of a brandy bottle.

For beasts of this nature—feed upon such poison, contorting and mutating with the newfound fuel.

Howling horribly and clawing with empty promises at my stomach lining.

Pining—craving as the vein does for a quick fix, providing some indulgence of the growing mental infection.

When nothing numbing is left, these persistent little parasites ravage their way through the melting muscle in my chest, past freshly forming breasts—till they dust their feet off on my common sense and swat at my synapses like string. Until, in time, they slow and sing:

> *"Oh, what sorrow you shall bring*
> *when to the fractured past we drink."*
> *For a second, my fingers flail to find my phone,*
> *and I remind you—I'm alone.*
> *[Cue the audience to groan]*
> *A well-known mistake*
> *made by the greatest of fakes*
> *with too much regret to finish the food on their plate.*
> *Guess it's better never—than too late.*

♡ AEG

Memories at Mealtime

About
the
Author

Gina Carrillo
aka Black Widow

Gina Carrillo is a Spoken Word Artist from Franklin, TN.
Creator of The Prodigal Poets Poetry Collective
Author of Kaleidoscope & Poets United, which can be found on Amazon
and Barnes & Noble websites.
Writings of love, loss, strength & resilience, overcoming death,
beating cancer, and domestic violence.

Peace, love & poetry.

Instagram: @blackwidowpoet @prodigalpoets
Facebook: Prodigal Poets or Black Widow & The Prodigal Poets & Black
Widow Poet

Demi Feeling
House of Pain
Lost Feeling
Gina Carrillo

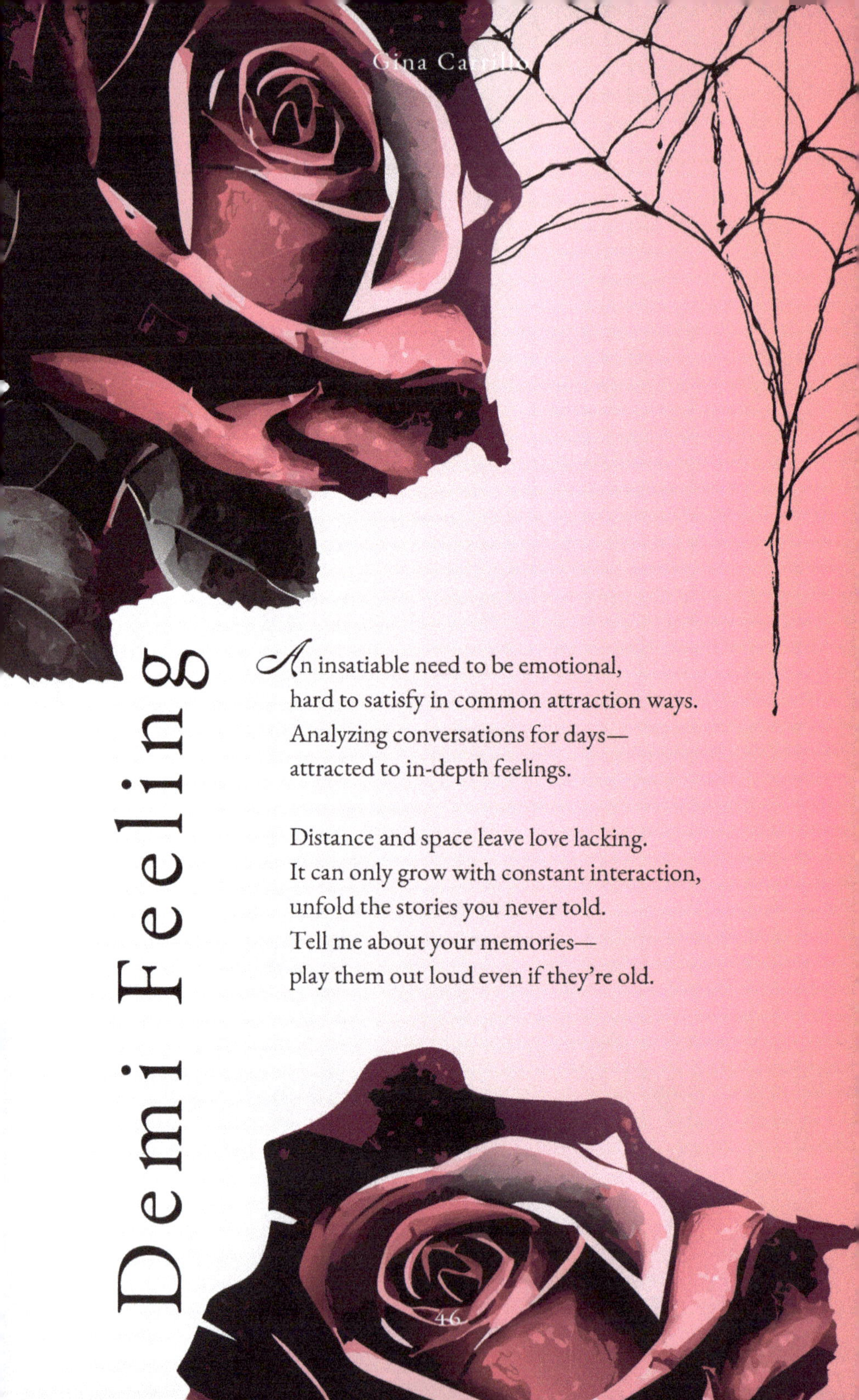

Demi Feeling

An insatiable need to be emotional,
hard to satisfy in common attraction ways.
Analyzing conversations for days—
attracted to in-depth feelings.

Distance and space leave love lacking.
It can only grow with constant interaction,
unfold the stories you never told.
Tell me about your memories—
play them out loud even if they're old.

Talk to me about questions that consume you—
getting to know yourself.
The fears you never told anyone else.
The things you never thought you would do.
The secrets that ruined your worldview.

Sometimes feeling broken,
I'm different than the rest.
Can we get to this place of familiarity?
Knowledge would need to be attained,
personality being highly entertained—
words flying smoothly and not strained.
Keep me reeling
give me some of that ***demi feeling***...

Black Widow

Gina Carrillo

House of Pain

*F*eeling like I could serve time in Arkham
with one more detrimental touch;
it would all be just too much—
pushing me over the ledge,
fighting Joker on the edge,
tired of this bad hand of poker.

While it's cold outside,
like ice crystallizing through my veins,
I'm scared I'll go insane
entering into the House of Pain—
not wanting to live a life in vain.

Past tragedies replay in my mind,
thinking about what I could do
differently every time.
Although I can't press **rewind.**

Hearing giggling sounds of laughter
all around;
I cry in despair
because I didn't get a happily ever after.

Just like Harley,
I'm starting to lose feelings,
but I'm breaking through glass ceilings
trying not to get cut.
Avoiding sinful interactions
much to my satisfaction.

This is just a preview
of my upcoming attraction;
although I saved a last dance—
may have one more bad romance...
What, really, would I gain
from living in this House of Pain?

Black Widow

Lost Feeling

Gina Carrillo

An unquenchable thirst for more
needed depth behind closed doors.
Difficult to satisfy in superficial ways—
philosophically thinking for days,
drawn to intellectual intricacies.

Time and thoughtlessness drains;
not enough to keep—mentally entertained.
Breadcrumbs will not satisfy me;
I'll need a feast of untold tales,
memories, and stories of the old version of you;
a play-by-play tale of your golden glory.

Discuss your thoughts with me;
questions that constantly flood your mind,
what you do in your free time,
the goals that you are working on yourself,
what makes you nervous and scared,
fears that you hide from everyone else...

The guilt and shame of something you did.
The past that ruined your love life.
Tell me about how that changed you.
Take me with you to enjoy your passions.
Indulge me with your favorite things.
Invite me to feel the joy it brings.

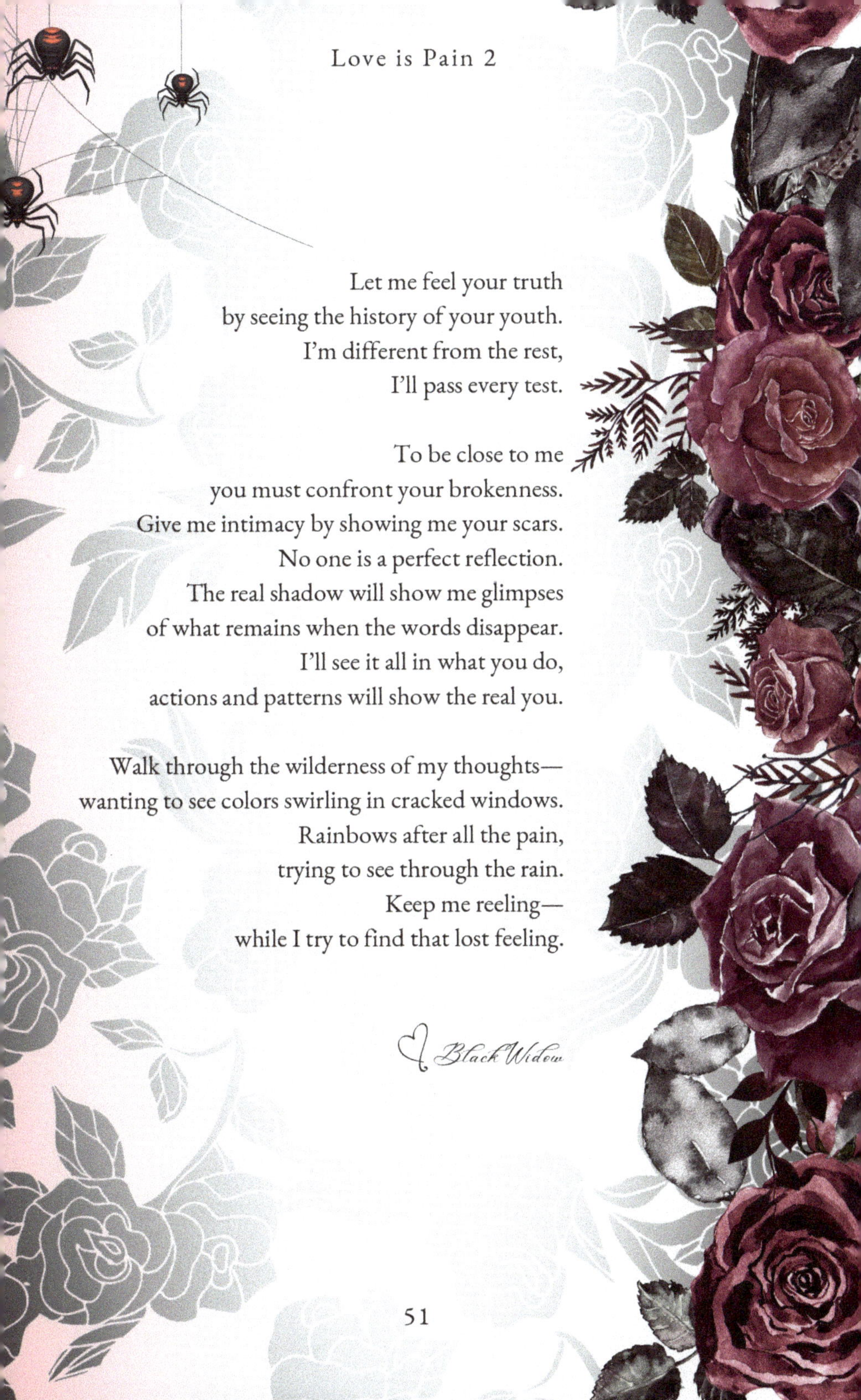

Let me feel your truth
by seeing the history of your youth.
I'm different from the rest,
I'll pass every test.

To be close to me
you must confront your brokenness.
Give me intimacy by showing me your scars.
No one is a perfect reflection.
The real shadow will show me glimpses
of what remains when the words disappear.
I'll see it all in what you do,
actions and patterns will show the real you.

Walk through the wilderness of my thoughts—
wanting to see colors swirling in cracked windows.
Rainbows after all the pain,
trying to see through the rain.
Keep me reeling—
while I try to find that lost feeling.

Black Widow

About the Author

Valerie Lorraine

Valerie Lorraine has 2 published books of her poetry collections, and 3 anthologies that include a healthy body of work from a total of 36 beautiful Poets. *Inked Inceptions, Prompted Conceptions* won the 2024 American Book Fest Award in the genre of Poetic Anthologies. Valerie continues to work on more books, which include both her personal work & anthologies.

Valerie works as an Editor, Writing Coach, and Self-Publishing Consultant. She also hosts a writing circle with The Federation of B.C. Writers. Her goal is to direct & encourage those who desire to create a legacy with their pen & their heart. She helps them bring their visionary art to life.

Valerie is extremely active as a host & mentor. She created a space specifically to support artists called Origin Of Thought on Instagram. This space can be found supporting many genres of shows and hosts on Instagram. Keep an eye out, there is always more coming! To find out more, Valerie Lorraine can be found on Instagram @valerielorraineproductions.

Books by Valerie can be found on Amazon at **amazon.com/author/valerie_lorraine**

Valerie Lorraine

Valerie Lorraine

It Wasn't Love

It wasn't love, it was rushed.
As your tongue licked my lips,
rushing my ears with your spells—
sticky sentiments adhering to my heart,
slowing each beat to your pace.

It wasn't love, it was sick.
Two lovers, in some kind of *dis-ease* state;
each not in love, first with ourselves,
breaking the rules of healthy affection.
You—just a fucking mess in every way,
and me—hoping love would cure,
ignoring the tower of madness
threatening to collapse on me.

It wasn't love, it was a game.
Manipulation for you to win.
My win was *love*.
Yours was getting me to never give up—
on you.

It wasn't love, it was trauma.
Two people with a cross to bear
came together, and sparks flew.
Romance and bad behaviour.
Let's be real, you dragged me down to your level,
I've spent years washing your bleeding pain off my soul.

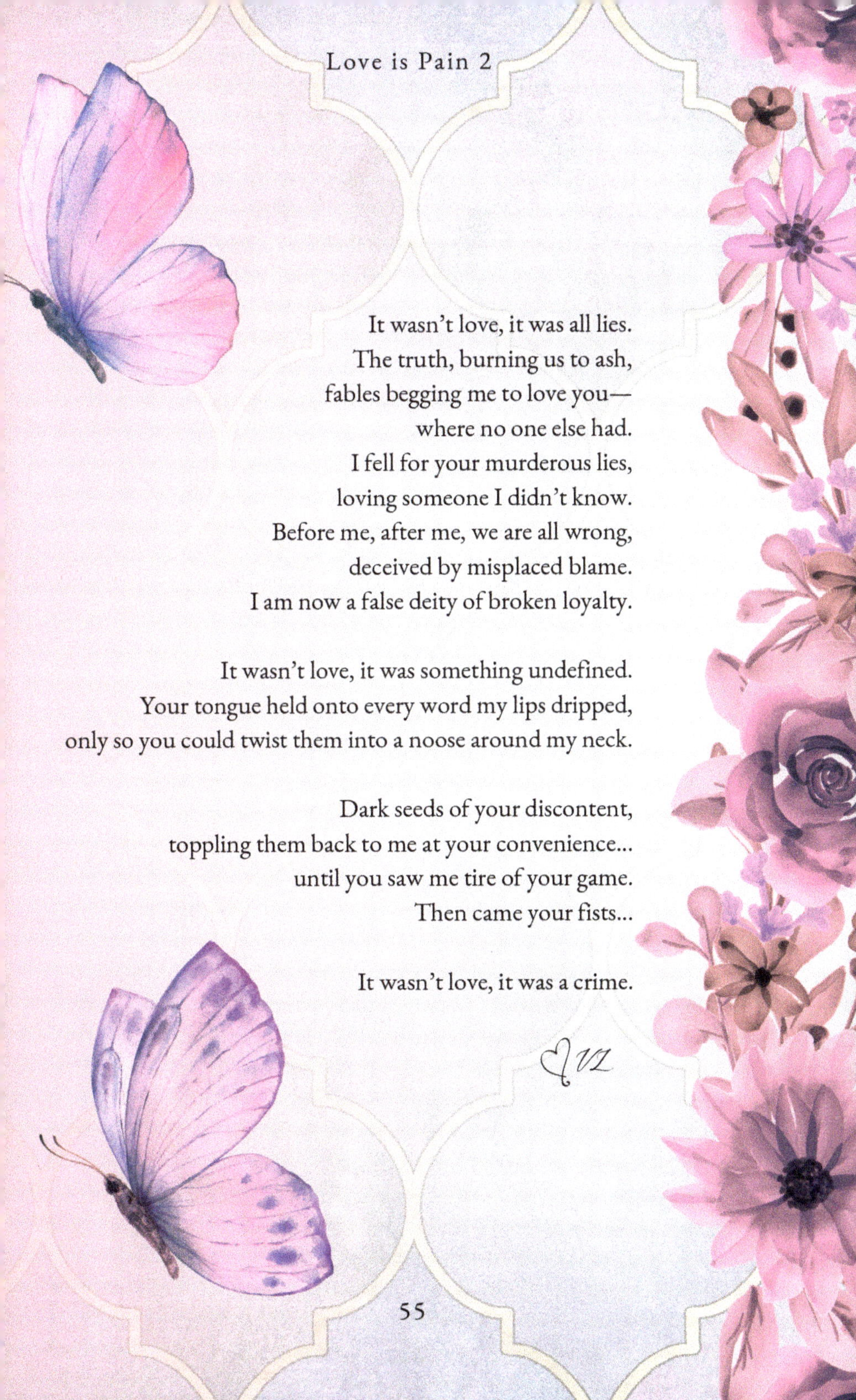

It wasn't love, it was all lies.
The truth, burning us to ash,
fables begging me to love you—
where no one else had.
I fell for your murderous lies,
loving someone I didn't know.
Before me, after me, we are all wrong,
deceived by misplaced blame.
I am now a false deity of broken loyalty.

It wasn't love, it was something undefined.
Your tongue held onto every word my lips dripped,
only so you could twist them into a noose around my neck.

Dark seeds of your discontent,
toppling them back to me at your convenience...
until you saw me tire of your game.
Then came your fists...

It wasn't love, it was a crime.

Valerie Lorraine

If you come looking, you'll find me.
A whispering ghost of passing hours.
To me, you are just someone I used to know.
Inoculated from the love you gave, the damage you caused.

So when you come looking, yes, you will find me—
at peace and still in the rain season,
whispering prayers as I push past the petrichor,
reaching for the sun when it finally glistens on my soul.

If you come, just come in dreams as the moon seeks destiny
and stars shake dust from their wishful tales.
I don't want to see you.
Whispers are all I have;
they become screams of colour
as I forcefully enter the cosmos.

Don't bring me to your thoughts,
I am beautiful where I am.
Your company is deafening to my whispers.
My life fell before its time.
I whisper louder.

Yes, you will find me
unrecognized amongst the stars,
bright, with a soft voice,
laughing and smiling with joy,
richly loud, auras of silky, vibrant hues,
passions of pink and lustered gold.

I am a ghost of your past;
I do not come to you or seek you.
Yet, you beckon me
as you wisp along your broken days.

I have been strawberry wine on your tongue,
whispered sacraments near your ears,
peacefulness to your broken soul,
and beauty to your thoughts.

All you may have of me is the ghost
whispering beside you;
the wild of intoxication.
I am very much alive— just not in your life.

I am your mind's ghost,
the ...fleeting ...whispering ...unattainable.

First published in *My Life... Untitled*

Synaesthesia

I awoke to the sound of dawn crackling.
Synaesthesia opened my heart—the blush of pink
clouding the surrounding Echos.

I will be there at sunset as the whisper of dusk enters.
I have found a new love—dark cresting,
the explosion of the starless night with no moon.

My awe shivers as the boom of ice slithers down an
Olympic blue mountain shelf—becoming the blame
for the resounding avalanche.

Slate skin, yellow corn husk voice,
encrypted hickory eyes, sprouting with wheat.

My love is the new black.
The unexpected hues become deafening.

♡ VL

First published in *My Life... Untitled*

How many times did I revisit the pain—
the anguish of the ways I grieved over you?

At one time, your breath near me was a sweet revelation;
a key, unlocking the feelings from captivity.
You masterfully cast a spell on me with your breath alone—
whispering across a delicate, immediate space;
a contagion, and a cure as unseen as the air in this room.

If only I could hold your breath to simply take one of my own,
allowing fresh, oxygenated thoughts to pursue a confused mind.
Breathe into my own capacity, and quiet my pleading heart.

I made a mistake— so many, in fact.

The countenance I made with blood was thicker
than the water of the womb,
and steadfast to unrequited loyalty.

I, in fact, forgot to breathe
in order to save myself.

First published in *Inked Inceptions, Prompted Conceptions*

The Act of Breathing

It Is Not You I Miss

Valerie Lorraine

It's not you I miss, it is the other you.
The one that you pretended to be.
The one that was intoxicating to my every breath.
The one that would have been enough
to calm the ache of my heart.
The one that would have warmed my cold, lonely soul.

I wanted to speak to you from my emotions,
gather all those thoughts that hold my heart in a guild.
I long to bade my words upon a string of ocean pearls,
their cream opacity lilting off my tongue;
expressing enough that you see my words,
feel my words—grasp you, and hold you.

I wanted to be your enough, washing you like ocean spray,
waves gently crashing in on your emotions, cold wash,
refreshing your sun-kissed skin on the hottest of days—
days made hot from the tempest, I am to you,
letting my words be the ecstasy you take,
swallowed back with warmed brandy—
getting drunk on each syllable as you kiss them off my lips.

Find the goddess hidden within as I travel among mere men.
All the gods seek to be worshipped,
yet you left my altar, barren and disrupted.
As you've found out,
as in any tale passed down through time,
a shunned god will quickly exile you.

Cold times found you as the prayers ceased.

Yes, gods, goddesses, we miss the heartbreak, the adore of men,
but men miss more of their gods once we are gone.

VL

First published in *My Life... Untitled*

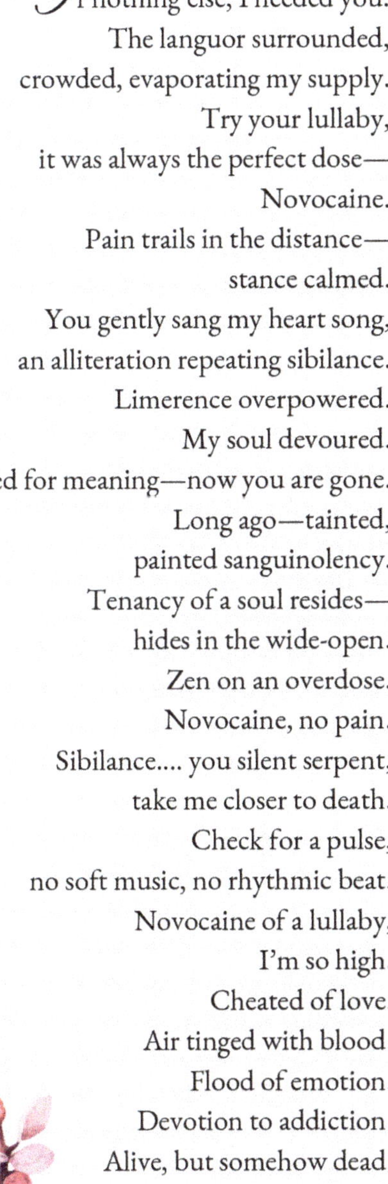

If nothing else, I needed you.
The languor surrounded,
crowded, evaporating my supply.
Try your lullaby,
it was always the perfect dose—
Novocaine.
Pain trails in the distance—
stance calmed.
You gently sang my heart song,
an alliteration repeating sibilance.
Limerence overpowered.
My soul devoured.
Scoured for meaning—now you are gone.
Long ago—tainted,
painted sanguinolency.
Tenancy of a soul resides—
hides in the wide-open.
Zen on an overdose.
Novocaine, no pain.
Sibilance.... you silent serpent,
take me closer to death.
Check for a pulse,
no soft music, no rhythmic beat.
Novocaine of a lullaby,
I'm so high.
Cheated of love.
Air tinged with blood.
Flood of emotion.
Devotion to addiction.
Alive, but somehow dead.

The Things I have Come to Know

Valerie Lorraine

I know you want me back.
Those quiet, sultry nights,
those moments you can't ever have again.
The hurt you must feel, the heartache of what you lost,
the pain of knowing how much I loved you—
and how you threw it all away.

Beautiful moments, watching the stars—
lost in moments like these.
Laughing, catching our breath, smiling
each time we looked into each other's eyes.
We made love in those moments—
our skin touched, our hearts locked.

I was a wildflower to your sunshine—
reaching up to feel the warmth.
I know you are missing me—
you can't hold back the wind!
You caused this storm;
inside of you it lived.
It lives on—in you,
and now in me.

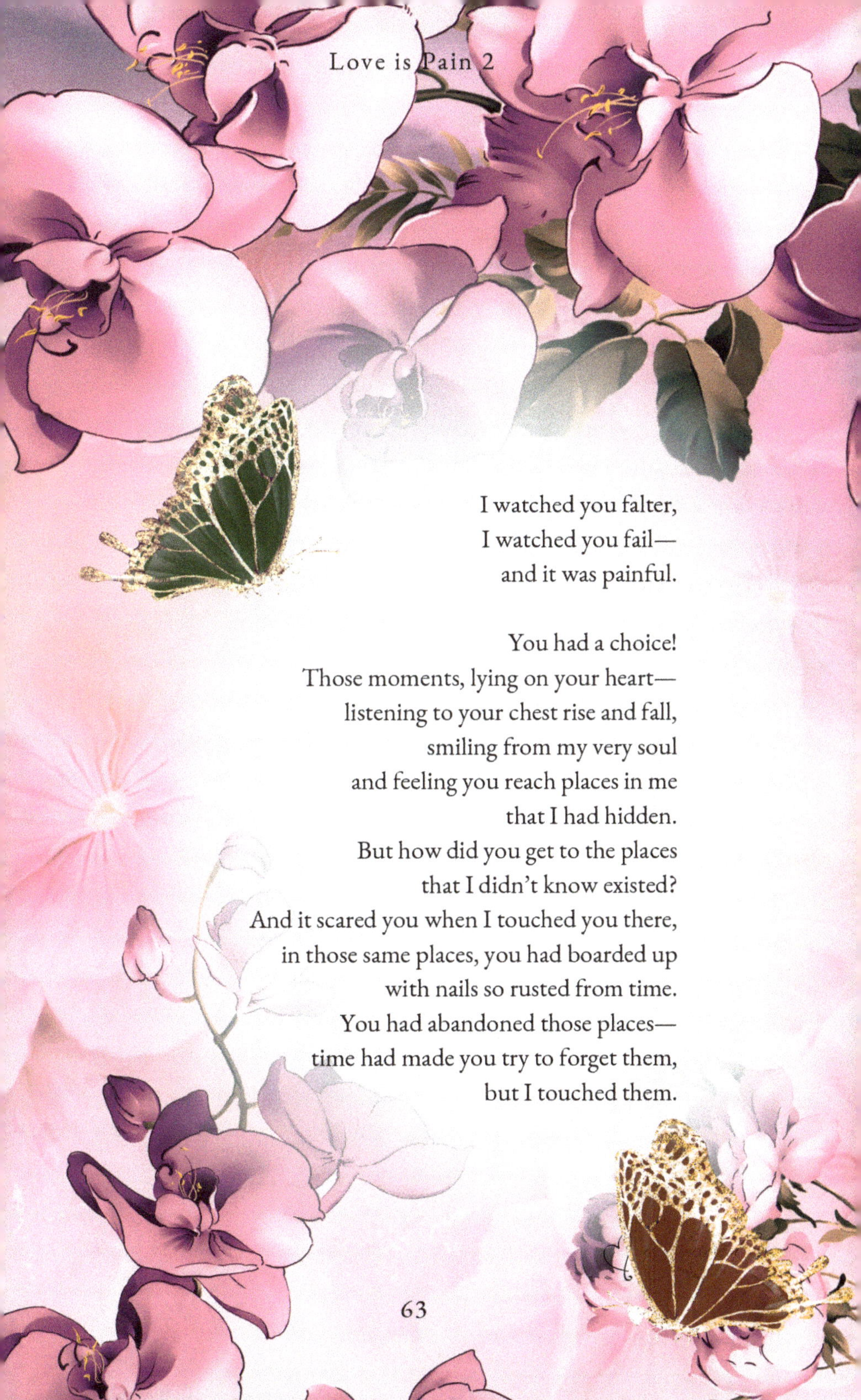

I watched you falter,
I watched you fail—
and it was painful.

You had a choice!
Those moments, lying on your heart—
listening to your chest rise and fall,
smiling from my very soul
and feeling you reach places in me
that I had hidden.
But how did you get to the places
that I didn't know existed?
And it scared you when I touched you there,
in those same places, you had boarded up
with nails so rusted from time.
You had abandoned those places—
time had made you try to forget them,
but I touched them.

I saw it shine through your eyes,
and at first, you loved it—
then I watched you forgo that love.
You chose to be a wild animal;
distancing yourself like I was a predator—
like I was a hunter.

You felt trapped by love.
Who does that?
You miss me now.
You know that hurting me was hurting you;
damaging you for all of eternity—
and all you have of me are memories.

The way that a lover
remembers holding that last embrace—
your fear became anger.

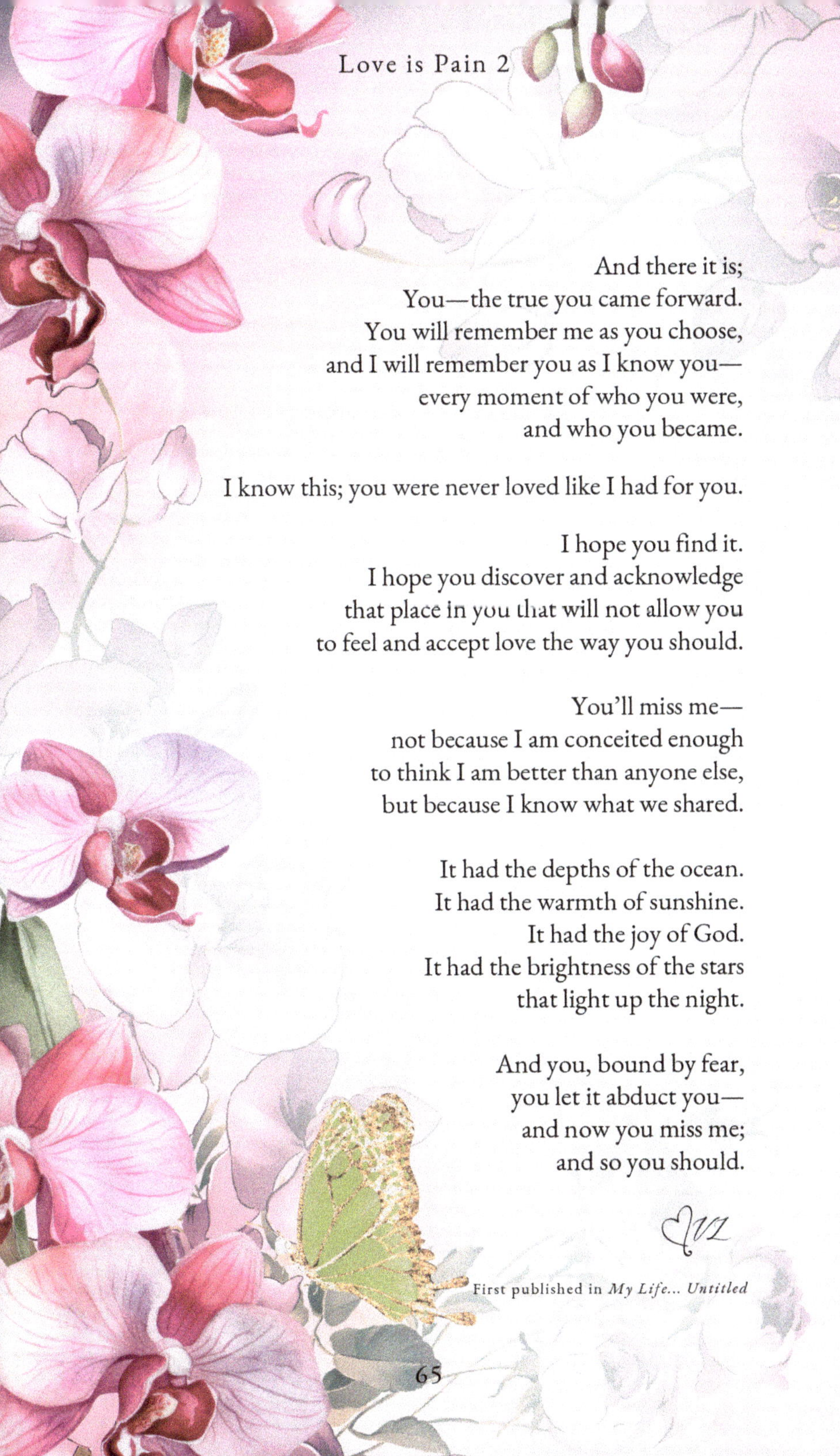

Love is Pain 2

And there it is;
You—the true you came forward.
You will remember me as you choose,
and I will remember you as I know you—
every moment of who you were,
and who you became.

I know this; you were never loved like I had for you.

I hope you find it.
I hope you discover and acknowledge
that place in you that will not allow you
to feel and accept love the way you should.

You'll miss me—
not because I am conceited enough
to think I am better than anyone else,
but because I know what we shared.

It had the depths of the ocean.
It had the warmth of sunshine.
It had the joy of God.
It had the brightness of the stars
that light up the night.

And you, bound by fear,
you let it abduct you—
and now you miss me;
and so you should.

First published in *My Life... Untitled*

Valerie Lorraine

Yours is the heart given, but not truly known.
And after all this time, how can love linger
in forgotten places?
And those not so forgotten...

A broken heart left in the gutter,
water rushing edges, sea glass nowhere near the sea.
A mermaid princess left out of water, to gasp—
accepting rain to flood her need for the ocean.

Heartstrings gently snipped as the mind recalls,
until the heart finally breaks free and severs from the soul.
An unkind gesture—the mind keeps you alive and well.

Love never dies, but the heart is murdered in heartbreak,
and yet never kills, reincarnated by memories carried
sweetly, softly, joyfully,
until they end in serial assassination.

Vocal cords cut off in violent pain, silence tastes
the calm in my mouth.
Words want to escape, only heard as animated breaths
of snowfall.

The Mindf*ck

My assassin's name is manipulation.
I found his signature etched quietly
behind words I'd hoarded in corners of memoirs,
reminders of human failure, the heart's pain.

The antidote is life, yet I cannot remain whole
to participate in drinking the elixir.
Death's head peaks and peers, ready to lunge,
slicing at my attempts to stitch my heart back into place.
I reached to return to the heavens you created in dreams
and awoke to the hell you birthed.

My wings suffer and char; chains bind my heart,
for which I can never leave...
I won't leave my suffering heart behind.

It appears the facade was heavenly.
I awoke from the mirage and must placate
as Satan sits to ponder with me.

Of all the journeys to be had with you,
this is the one I want to have not taken.

I marinated myself in the beauty of your spices.

The aromas of you saturated my senses,
until it settled in my brain,
so memories evoked easily as I caught you in the air I breathe in.

There you are in my thoughts:
yester-year,
yesterday,
and hopeful for tomorrow.

The air is warm and damp from sea spray,
as you walked hand in hand with me.

Our footprints, temporary in the wet sands,
water pulling proof of our path back to the rolling waves.

I long for your hand to reach for mine again,
as my hair absorbs the sea salt carried on the blowing breeze.

Time cannot hold you back from me;
it can only distance us along the horizon.

Painfully, I wait for you
and your reaching hand.

The ocean has been my favourite place,
where you etched our initials in the large deadwood
now bleached from the sun.

Marinated

I still wear the beach glass you gave me,
harnessed in wire by your strong hands,
and laced with leather; you tied it around my neck.

My fingers play along the soft edges.
It won't cut my hand,
but it jaggedly daggers into my heart,
just lying so near its rhythmic beat.

The glistening sun lies bronze on my skin,
as it plays with reflective light over the washing blue water.

My feet sink deeper;
I push them down hard
in a desperate attempt to let the earth know
I will not give in.
I will not give in.

I will wait, because I know you are there
on the other side of that ocean,
calling for me
on tidal winds that cast your voice in whispers.

So I will come every sunset when the tide is out,
and hope to see your footprints
pathing their way to me.

First published in *My Life... Untitled*

Tiger Eyes with all those Lies

Valerie Lorraine

You paraded into my life.
You took me like a storm takes the ocean
and makes hurricanes,
and with all your deceit, you tore up my life.

I loved you,
with all my soul and all my being.
I gave all of myself to you;
I didn't save anything for anyone else.

You demanded it of me silently,
like the rain demands that everything it touches
gets sodden with its strength—
sometimes calm, sometimes violent.

And that was you:
unpredictable.

You are a drug,
and you intoxicated my very soul.

My life was addicted to you—
toxic and wasteful,
not a life,
but a dream.

And the visions you created were not a reality:
just an oasis,
an aura,
a facade.

Love is Pain 2

My reality is me, and here I am,
learning that all lies carry an ounce of truth.

Your truth is that there is nothing left of you.

You are a beautiful shell on the beach,
that is vacant of an inhabitant.
You want to pick it up and keep it,
but it is empty and soulless.

If you put it to your ear, you can hear the ocean,
and it gives you hope, and your dreams come alive.
Then you remember that it is your blood
rushing through your body that you hear,
and not really the ocean. Another lie.

Then the power comes:
I know that I am the love I felt,
and you pulled it from me like a wave, like that storm,
so that you could feel alive.

But it is my blood, and my storm,
and I rage in the wind and the rain,
and I will keep that forever.

My love is not yours.
You didn't deserve it,
you didn't earn it truthfully,
and for that, I will forever be safe in the storm.

First published in *Falling*

71

Valerie Lorraine

*Y*ou were my favourite colour.

I was 'I'm in for love' pink,
and you were 'chocolate drizzle' brown.

When our colours collided on the page,
I would smile, my matrix glitching wildly.

Together we made a colour
close to one in the box called 'On fire for you.'

My lines were always crisp and detailed,
ready to smudge the edges to soften the look of my picture.

And you always ran your colour right along the outlines.
The page, wet from the oil pastels.

I'd often draw something we saw
when we were out making the most of life:
like the American Paint horses,
eating over-ripened apples ready to drop from the trees
as they reached up atop the raggedy fence.

The streaking sun found ways to break between the leaves,
or the moon balancing in the sky over the rippled water,
bouncing with light glitter
as we stood on the grass near the railway tracks.

When we drove home, I squeezed my eyes shut
and took a picture of it in detail
with my photographic memory.

Our song played loudly as we sang each of our parts
of the duet 'If it's meant to be,'
while my feet, as the song says, rested on the dash.

Pastels

We were so perfect when we were together,
romantic, blissful, and comfortably at ease.

It was when I wasn't there that you coloured outside the lines.
I never saw the picture you were drawing,
or I would have seen more than just us in the frame.
I probably would have seen my broken heart
drawn in shades of 'shamed ego pink' off to the side.

But you didn't show me what you were drawing.
Instead, you let me draw your portrait in charcoal,
soft lines with your hands praying,
while I got my fingers all stained, blending the oils
against the stark white textured paper.

Your gentle drawl and the way you enunciated your A's
elicited smiles I hid behind my coffee cup.
The closer you got to me for that gateway kiss,
the stronger I sensed your pheromones overwhelming my
subconscious.
That is where love bloomed for me,
while colouring flowers with pastels
named 'embarrassed blue,' 'red flags,' 'gullable grey,'
'jaded green,' and 'da-pressed lavender,'
wondering, 'Who named these colours?'

As I flip through that old art book,
I realize that whoever named that box of pastels
was someone just like me.

First published in *My Life... Untitled*

Valerie Lorraine

I remember the first time I saw the magic of fireflies,
on a road trip at a rest-stop in the Midwest,
amongst the lavender skies of a heated summer night.

My excitement was childlike and untamed,
as I confined the light in the safety of my widely cupped hands.
I held that light in captivity for as long as I could,
letting my heart secretly pump chanted spells
within the beats to keep this moment alive forever.

As all good things come to an end, I slowly peeled back my fingers,
releasing the little lantern from within my capture.
I watched as the light floated towards the other glistening life
near a split tree hit by lightning from yesterday's storm.

Graffiti on the cement bath house gave the feel
of urban walls hosting Thoughts by Steve:
He wrote, 'Steve loves Jada forever.'
Did he really? I wondered. And how much?

I remember thinking
how much I thought you might love me
as you bent to lay butterscotch kisses on my lips.

Fireflies

The candy I bought you at the market earlier,
 now wedged within your cheek,
the slight bulge, giving up its hiding place.

We watched the butterfly moths
and lightning bugs well into the depths of dusk.
The embers of their flight became my only hope
that this would not end.

 And as if on cue, the stars lit up the sky
as the roaring hues of the final shiver of sunset dove into
dulled darkness.

What I remember most is the joy I felt
and how close we were without the distractions of others.
Those fairytale moments made it so painfully hard when
it was time to say a final goodbye to you.

First published in *My Life... Untitled*

About the Author

Gary S. Watkins

Gary considers himself more of a dabbler than a true poet or writer. Nevertheless, getting to see his work out in the world still brings a bit of a thrill with it. His poetry has appeared in Star*Line, the "Tis the Season" Anthology from Red Penguin Publishing, Three Line Poetry, Anthology in Aid of Guide Dogs for the Blind, Poetry Soup, and various blogs.

Attribution: Walking Away was previously published on 02/03/2014 in the Writing Through Your Divorce Blog; http://writingdivorce.com/the-blog/

The Waning
Hurting
Walking Away
Gary S. Watkins

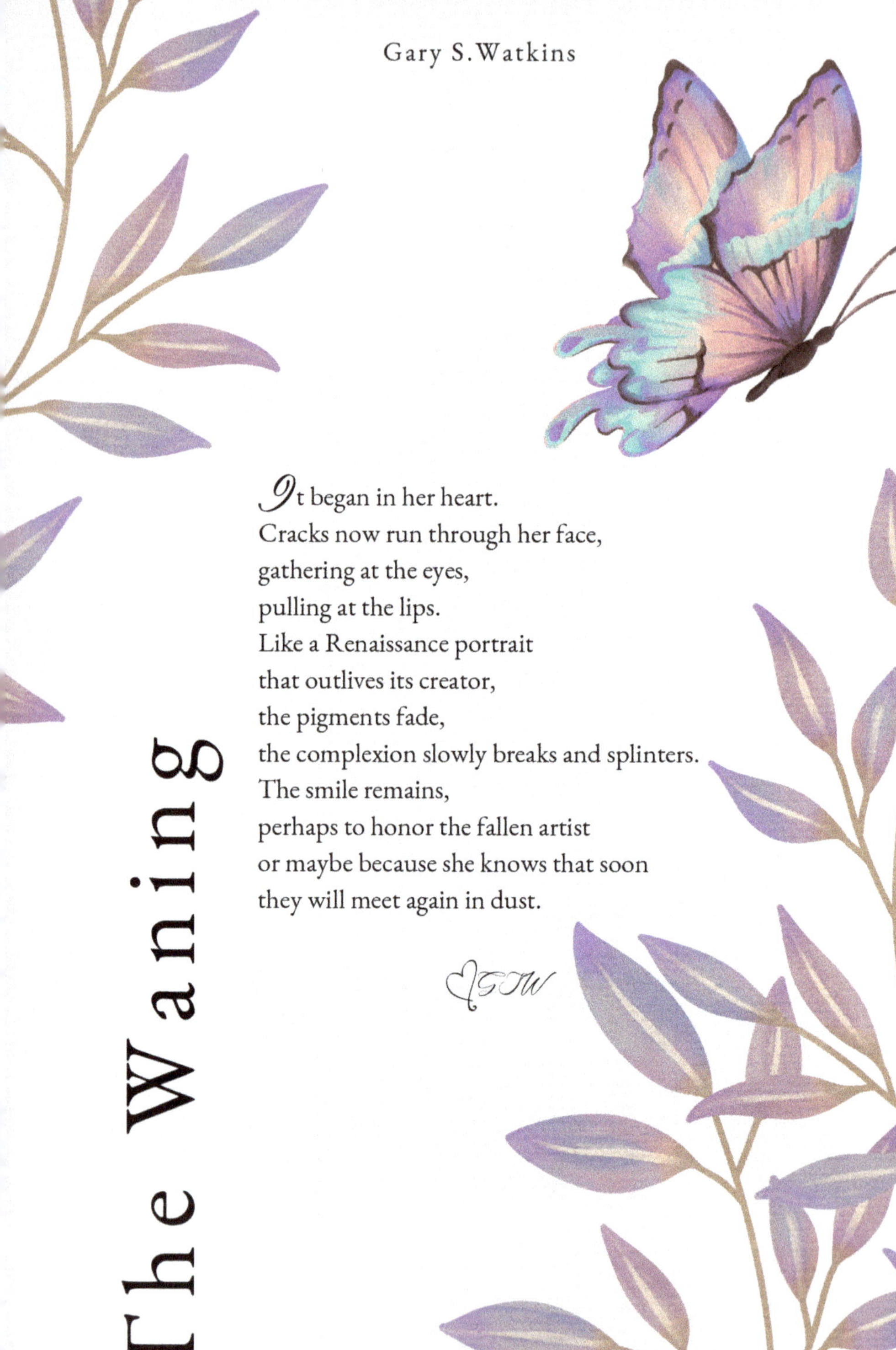

Gary S. Watkins

The Waning

It began in her heart.
Cracks now run through her face,
gathering at the eyes,
pulling at the lips.
Like a Renaissance portrait
that outlives its creator,
the pigments fade,
the complexion slowly breaks and splinters.
The smile remains,
perhaps to honor the fallen artist
or maybe because she knows that soon
they will meet again in dust.

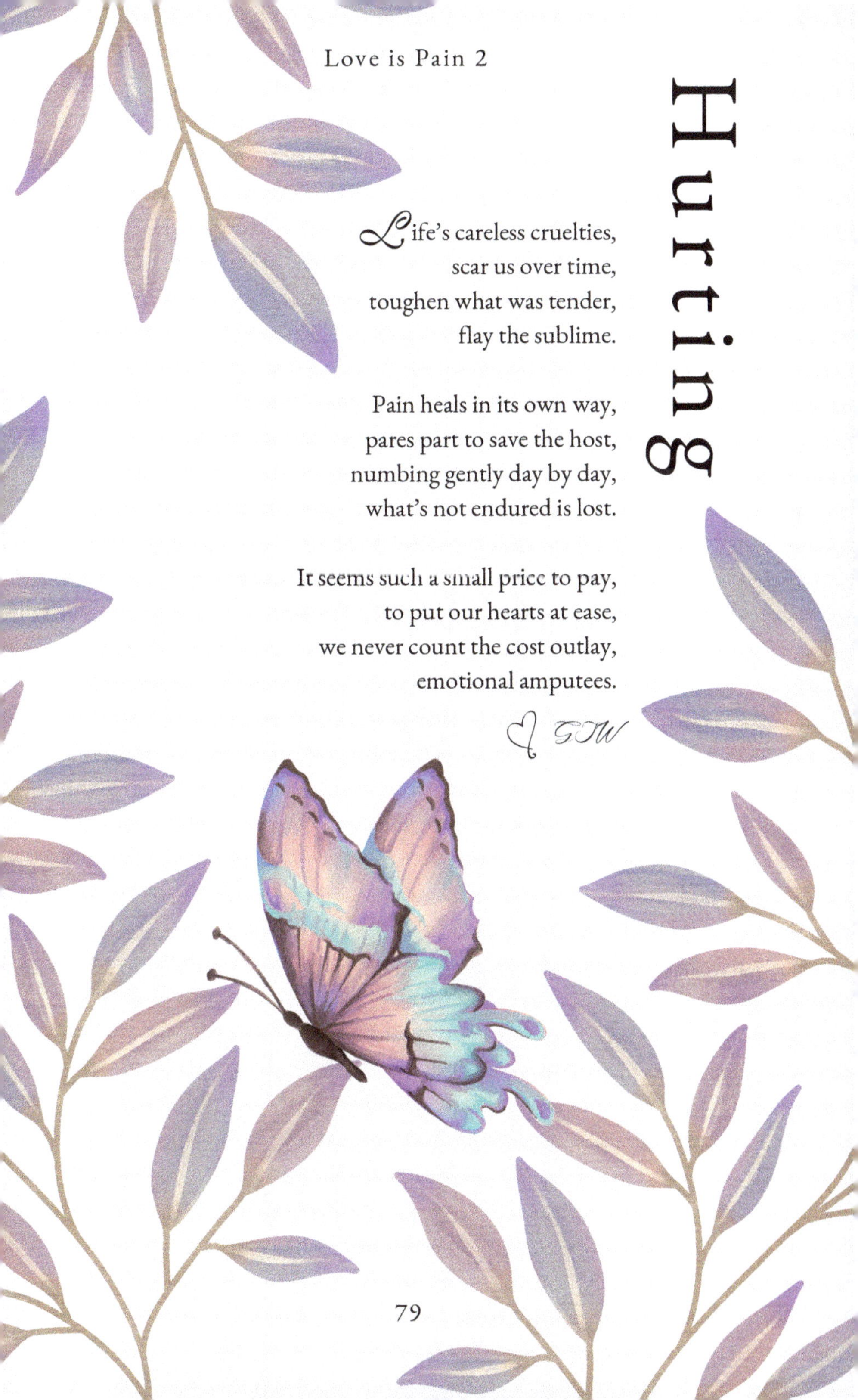

Hurting

*L*ife's careless cruelties,
scar us over time,
toughen what was tender,
flay the sublime.

Pain heals in its own way,
pares part to save the host,
numbing gently day by day,
what's not endured is lost.

It seems such a small price to pay,
to put our hearts at ease,
we never count the cost outlay,
emotional amputees.

♡ GW

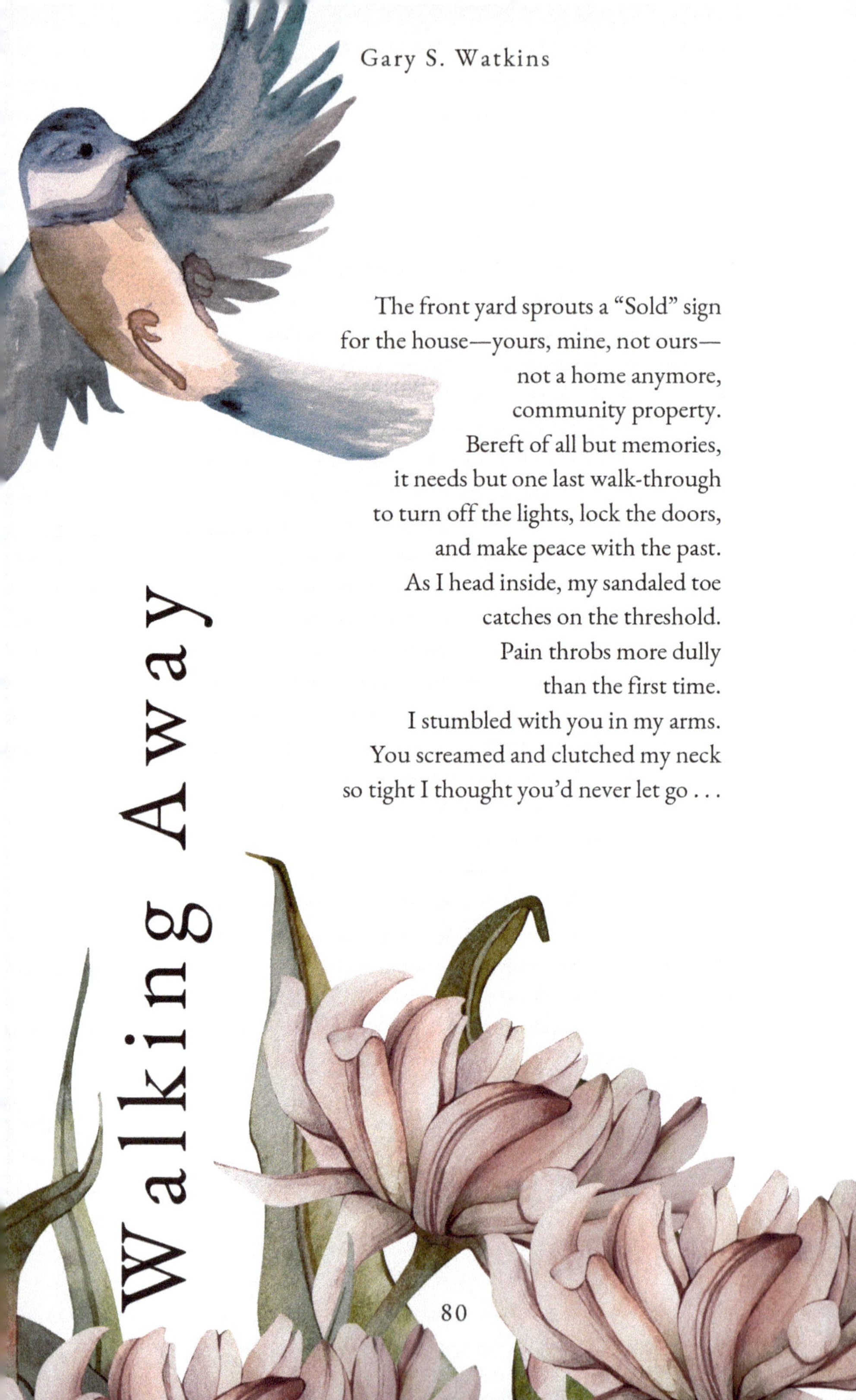

Gary S. Watkins

The front yard sprouts a "Sold" sign
for the house—yours, mine, not ours—
not a home anymore,
community property.
Bereft of all but memories,
it needs but one last walk-through
to turn off the lights, lock the doors,
and make peace with the past.
As I head inside, my sandaled toe
catches on the threshold.
Pain throbs more dully
than the first time.
I stumbled with you in my arms.
You screamed and clutched my neck
so tight I thought you'd never let go . . .

Walking Away

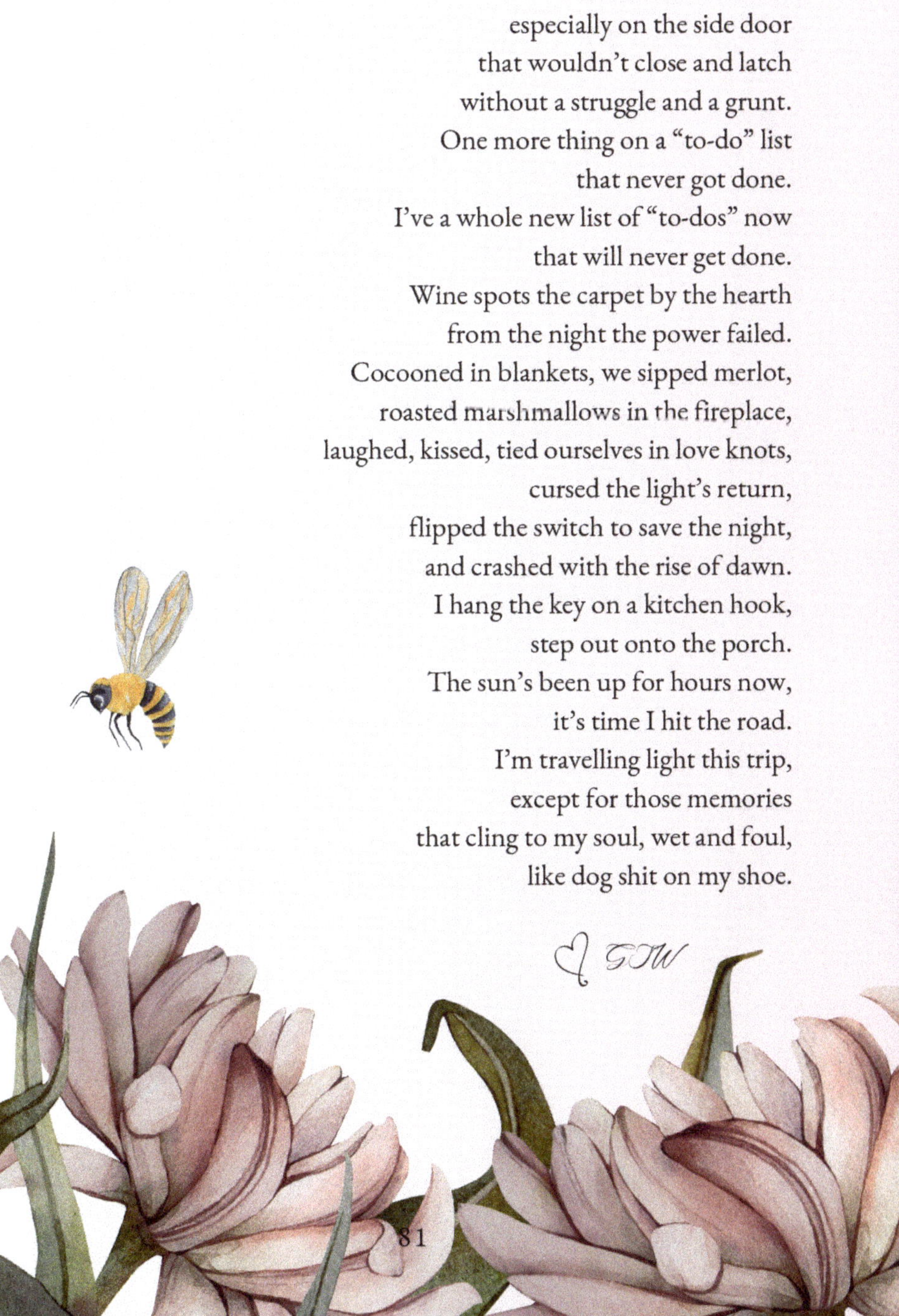

. . . I was wrong.
I shut the windows, check the locks,
especially on the side door
that wouldn't close and latch
without a struggle and a grunt.
One more thing on a "to-do" list
that never got done.
I've a whole new list of "to-dos" now
that will never get done.
Wine spots the carpet by the hearth
from the night the power failed.
Cocooned in blankets, we sipped merlot,
roasted marshmallows in the fireplace,
laughed, kissed, tied ourselves in love knots,
cursed the light's return,
flipped the switch to save the night,
and crashed with the rise of dawn.
I hang the key on a kitchen hook,
step out onto the porch.
The sun's been up for hours now,
it's time I hit the road.
I'm travelling light this trip,
except for those memories
that cling to my soul, wet and foul,
like dog shit on my shoe.

♡ GJW

About
the
Author

S.D. Kilmer

S. D. Kilmer has poetry published in a variety of literary anthologies (The Poet/Robin Barratt Publications, Wheelsong Press, SweetyCat Press, Author PressUK, MacKenzie Publishing). His poetry has also appeared in various online literary journals (SpillWords, MasticadoresUSA, Severance Magazine, Poetry for Mental Health, among others). His own electronic journal is Emergence Journal at SDKilmer.com. Residing in Syracuse NY, the author founded on Facebook "The Poets of New York State" group. He retired from roles as a Pastoral Counselor and Family Mediator. S.D. Kilmer passed away August 17, 2025. He leaves behind two adult sons whom he loved dearly.

Every Man for Every Woman

No Tree

Wedding Photos

How Blue

Give You My Love

Little Bit of Love

S.D. Kilmer

S.D. Kilmer

Every Man For Every Woman

Whenever it rains.
Whenever there's pain.
When the days are all the same.
When he's feeling pretty lame,
there's always a woman who loves him.

Through the highs and lows of life.
Through the grief and times of relief.
Through his youth, into his golden years.
There's always a woman who'll soothe his fears.

John and Yoko were a rare duo.
George and Olivia were blessed from the start.
Richie and Barbara, Paul and Linda,
well, love was love for them no doubt.

I never found my anam cara.
And I cry when I'd rather shout.

I've had escapades. Oh, how I've paid.
I've had my preoccupations and obsessions,
and I've had a love that lasted for twenty-two years—
but hers lasted for only two.
What was a man to do?

Then there are women
who have a man to stand
in equal support.
Good for them!

But I've seen men
playing with her affection,
betraying her dedication.
In his eyes, she never sees it coming.

Where is this woman for every man?
Every man for a woman.
Such absurdity, you see!
.

♡ JDK

S.D. Kilmer

I was thrown out, from on high,
from the last standing tree in the sky.
Ripped from my roots,
couldn't even say "goodbye."
Cut to the core,
I had no myth or lore.
I no longer could see
which branch was mine.

No trees.
No origins.
No family.
No family of trees.
No tree of families.
No family trees.
Nor roots.
Just a false narrative told to me,
and a pair of boots; but,
no tree for this Kilmer.

JDK

No Tree

Wedding Photos

*M*uch likened to the marriage,
all the wedding photos are gone;
shredded and discarded
as the relationship itself.

The wedding. The day I wept.
I wept, while she was thrilled—
and the priest blessed us.
Did he bless my tears?
I never could believe through all my fears.

Why it took twenty years to pry us apart
when we had existentially separated already, you see?

Understanding has always eluded me.
We came together as mutual support.
as we ventured out into the wild world.
Then, we remained until we fell apart
and became a relationship—
shredded and discarded.

S.D. Kilmer

How Blue

(For Jackson C. Frank)

I heard your first love
extinguished by fire.
You flew to London,
you met there, Paul Simon.
Whiskey and gin to wash the blues each day—
she's on your mind,
splitting you in a few ways.
Whenever you're thinkin' or not sleepin'
you've felt lovin' and livin' is all a game.
How blue can you be?

All experience seems to be the same.
You've seen all the world blue.
Lost another love, and a son.
Wherever you've gone you've never won.
As you look up from your depths,
how blue can you be?

How blue can you have been?
You lay down in your hometown,
Buffalo can be a cold place, too.
Oh how blue there, will you be?

Give You My Love

Before I open my heart to you,
will your own heart be true?
Been down this road before,
heartbreak I desire no more.

Before I take your hand,
I've been in love before.
I got backed out of her door.
She was never "in love", and nothing more.

Before I walk over that bridge with you,
from love's start to life's end,
I need to know we will always be more than friends—
so I can give you my heart, anew.

Before I can give you my love,
I need to know your love is plain;
no complications or complexities,
from all of which, is too much pain.

Were I to love you,
I must know
if your love is unending.
Just as Love itself— is eternal expending.

♡ JDK

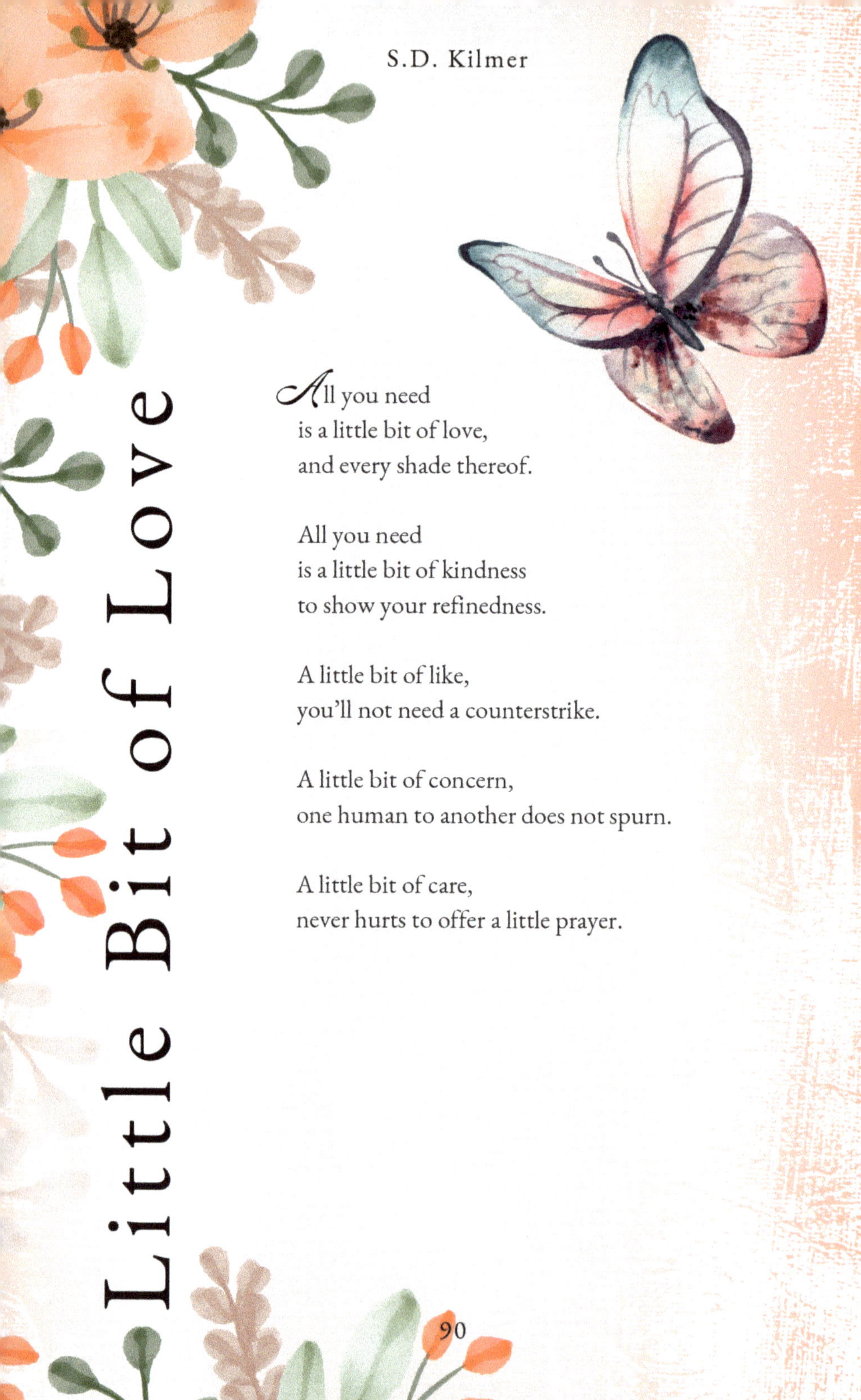

S.D. Kilmer

All you need
  is a little bit of love,
  and every shade thereof.

All you need
  is a little bit of kindness
  to show your refinedness.

A little bit of like,
  you'll not need a counterstrike.

A little bit of concern,
  one human to another does not spurn.

A little bit of care,
  never hurts to offer a little prayer.

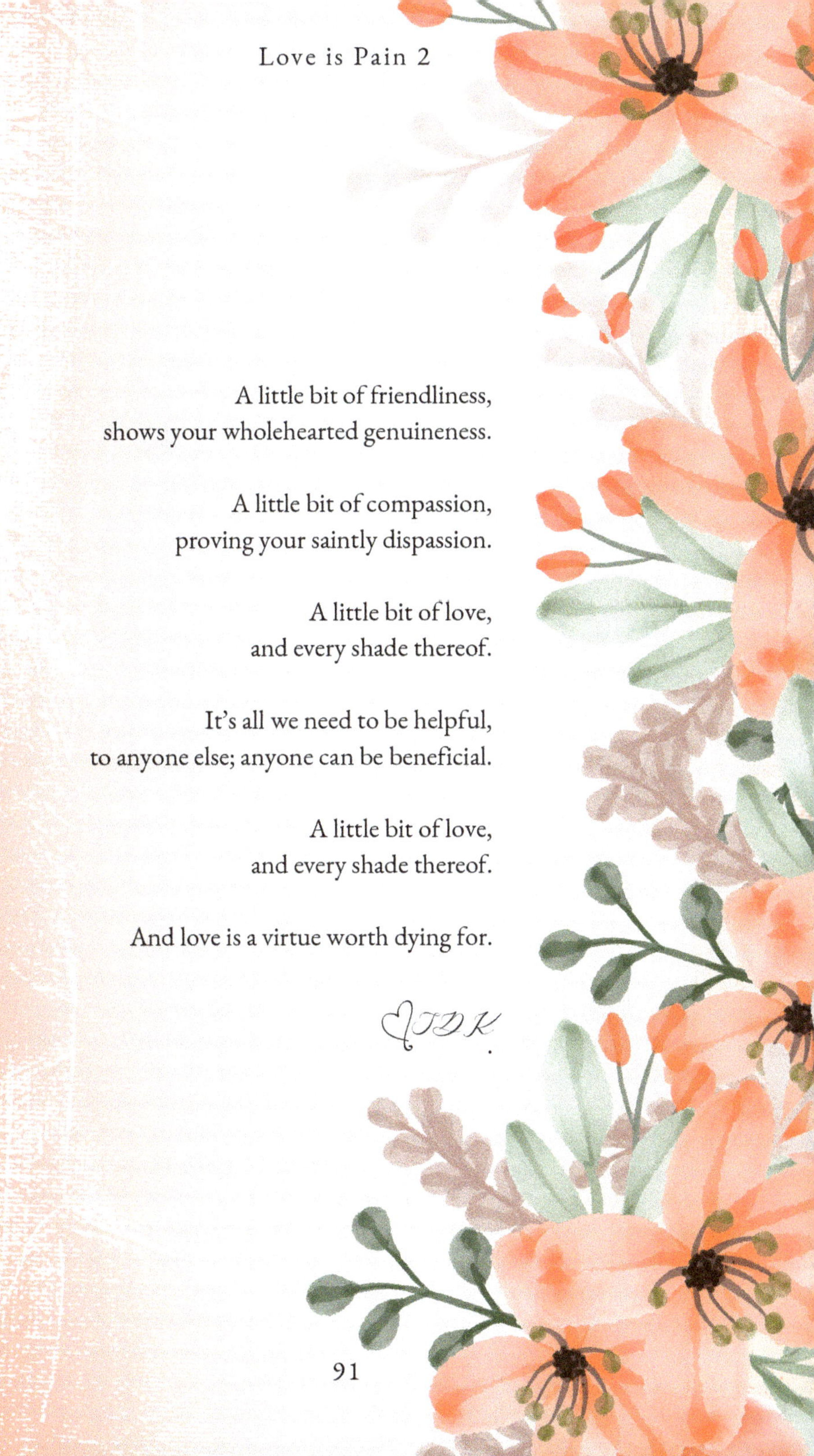

A little bit of friendliness,
shows your wholehearted genuineness.

A little bit of compassion,
proving your saintly dispassion.

A little bit of love,
and every shade thereof.

It's all we need to be helpful,
to anyone else; anyone can be beneficial.

A little bit of love,
and every shade thereof.

And love is a virtue worth dying for.

About
the
Author

Joshua Robinson

Joshua Robinson received degrees in Playwriting and Poetry from the University of Missouri; they went on to complete a Master's of Arts Management at Columbia College Chicago.

They have performed nationally and locally, both theatrically, poetically, and somewhere in between. Their work has been featured or is forthcoming in *The Maneater*, *The Vail Mountaineer*, *Newcity*, *Life and Literature in Performance*, *Mizzou New Play Festival*, *The Edge Theatre*, *CommuterLit*, *microstory.me*, *Hemingway's Playpen*, Spit Poet Zine, Boulder Poetry Scene's, I Love Your Poem, and more.

Joshua runs The Stand Open Mic at the Coffee Stand every second Friday of the month. Joshua's first book of poetry "This Way to Exit, Millennialism, and New Poems." is available online, at local bookstores, and personally from the author. Their memoir, "Homeless with God" is forthcoming.

Joshua Robinson

Joshua Robinson

My heart came from the trees
long before there was anything
confusing about being an adult.

I was given a thousand rings
in a severed limb, and now I
can prove that I am timeless.

Someday this will all be firewood,
but I don't own a cabin, and
that too came from Earth long

before we showed up to cut
down trees that no longer sing.
Please, listen to the sounds of

Wooden

missiles, and the shockwave of an
explosion that cannot be felt,
because it rips through your

skin and tears apart the pieces of you
that used to be made of wood.
Here put your head against the

Earth and listen to the sounds
of a thousand bison dying for
sport, not for food, not for

spirituality, not for science,
but just because we are sick,

broken and melting like a
candle. I don't have a solution
for you. I don't have a way
for you to look into the

continued

Joshua Robinson

future. I've already been there.
Know that it's not as bad as
you think. There are still trees here

there are still elements passed
down from aspen to aspen.
It's okay to consume, everything

must stay alive. You're not here
to be an aesthete, devoid of desire
and impulse. We are still flesh, brain,

and branches of the Oort Cloud
that have slid down to the soil.
Look out for neon, flowing

through the veins of an oak. This
all comes back to you standing
in front of a dying building,

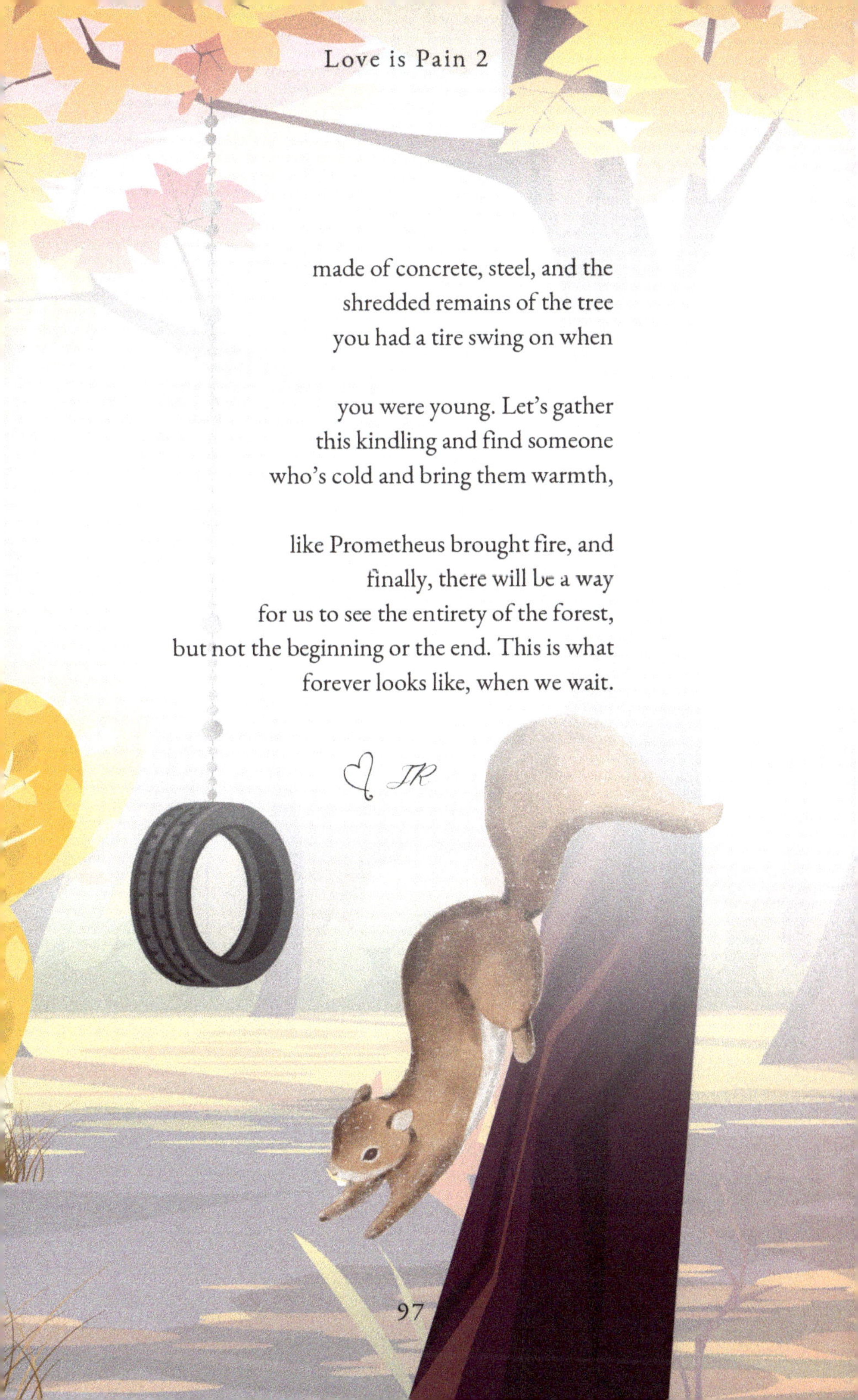

made of concrete, steel, and the
shredded remains of the tree
you had a tire swing on when

you were young. Let's gather
this kindling and find someone
who's cold and bring them warmth,

like Prometheus brought fire, and
finally, there will be a way
for us to see the entirety of the forest,
but not the beginning or the end. This is what
forever looks like, when we wait.

About the Author

George Oberg

George Oberg was born and grew up in Los Angeles, California. He is a Marine Corps and Coast Guard veteran, he currently works in the healthcare field. George has been writing since his early teens. He currently lives in Northern Ohio. His poetry has been featured in other anthologies such as *The Fall and Rise of Chimeras, Grey, We Hide Our Colors Within Vol. 1, Wild Butterflies,* and *Instagram Poets You'll Want To Follow.* George is an avid reader of science-fiction and fantasy mystery. George loves to karaoke, and can often be found, diving into rabbit holes, seeking truth, or spending time in his vegetable Garden. He is the father of two grown children. He currently lives alone, the caretaker of four feline overlords. In moments of solitude, George writes what he feels, or what he sees in this great big world, or simply to make sense of the world we live in.

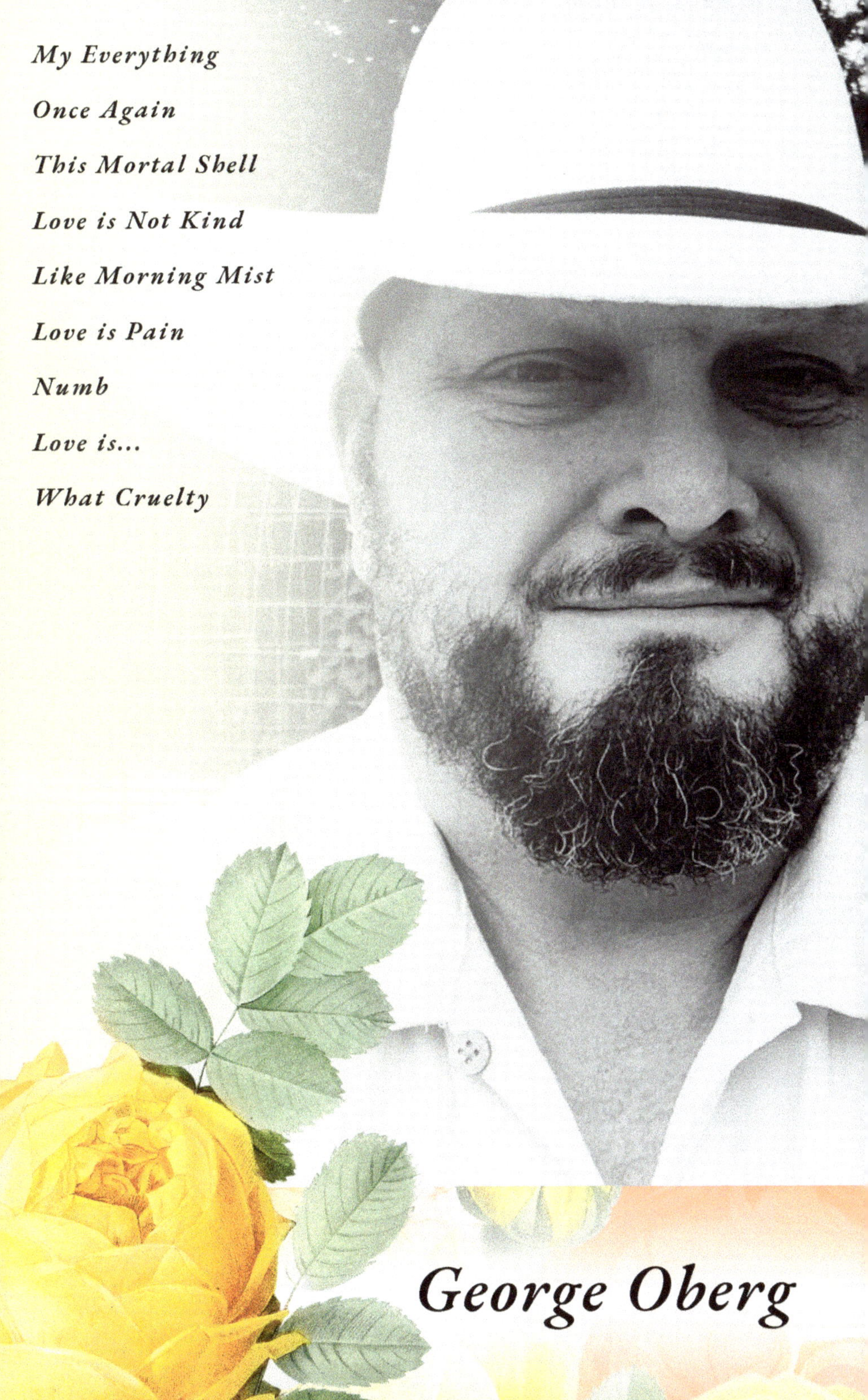
My Everything
Once Again
This Mortal Shell
Love is Not Kind
Like Morning Mist
Love is Pain
Numb
Love is...
What Cruelty
George Oberg

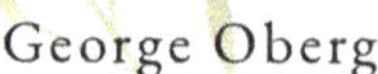

She said, "I want to be your everything"
I moved heaven and earth
Put her at the center of my universe
Opened my soul
Showed her
She was my heart
My hopes
My dreams
My home
My love
Then she left
Taking only one thing
My everything

My Everything

I lay numb to the pain
Opened my heart
For it was locked
A fortress under siege
But you I gave the key
Never knowing the assassin
Come in the night
A dagger thrust
Piercing my happiness
My hopes
My dreams
Dumbfounded
Fingers laced I bleed
Through hands
Not meant to bind my own pain
Eviscerating my soul
Skillfully struck
The light in my eyes fading
Falling in love my sin
Both living and dead
Once again

Once Again

This Mortal Shell

I miss the love I saw there
In your beautiful eyes
I found paradise
My heart beating with joy
All my dreams come to fruition
You were love
You were my love
My home
My world
Our Eden
Poisoned Doubt and fear
Not true orientation
Now I stand
The edge of devastation
Everything in ruination
My world a garden of stones
Dead and dying
Eternal winter fills my soul
Dreams shattered
Devoid of all hope
Powerless
All I can do is cry
As my world crumbles
The cold seeps inside
Into my heart
Chilling me
Killing me I am no Lazarus
There is no resurrection
There is only pain
Absolve me of my sin of living
Release me from this prison
This life
This hell
This mortal shell

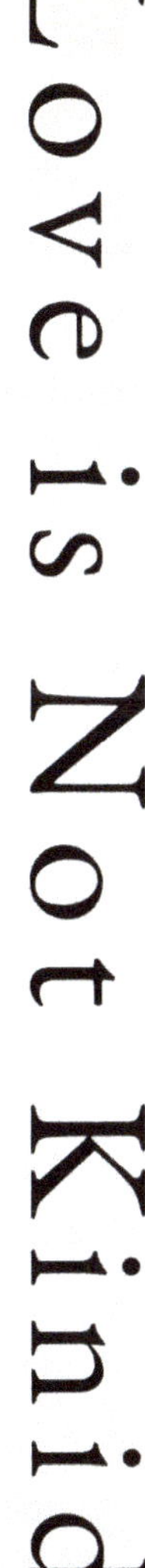

Love is not kind It is not sweet
It's a darkened soul
A savage beast
It taunts you
Whispered sweet nothings
Tells you somebody wants you
When you finally believe
It rips you
Tears you apart
Paralyzed
It shreds your heart
Then it forever haunts you

George Oberg

I remember love
Like morning mist dissipating in the sun
Chasing unicorns
Trying to trap that dream magic
Moments of passion
Kissing
A home for my heart
A loving companion
Early dawn light illuminates the sky
Grasping vainly
I try
Oh how I try
Holding onto wispy moments of happiness
Onto those beautiful feelings
Then I awaken
Reality hits
The passion
The home for my heart
The loving companionship
The happiness
The beautiful feelings
They don't mean a thing
I didn't
Love like a unicorn is just a dream
It doesn't really exist
It fades to the rising Sun
Like morning mist

Oh how
We loathe being told you're such a nice guy
You're a good man
I love how we are such good friends
They tell you what they want
Describe you in every way
How they wish they could find that man
Inside your head
Screaming here I fucking am
But never you
You're just a friend
Do you even know how painful
Soul crushing that can be
Asking time after time why not me
Seeing them choose those who hurt them
And when the tears flow
At the next heartbreak
To you they run
Your shoulder to cry on
Never knowing inside you too are breaking
Your heart is aching
You pick up your own pieces
You paste theirs back with tender care
But in the shadows
The slow death of the good man
With each I wish I could find someone like you
Till the good man is gone
Always on the sidelines
Always left perplexed
Left behind
Love unrequited his slayer
Where once a good man stood a heartless player.
Can you feel yourself dying
Stripped layer by layer
Never hearing your name
Knowing only love is pain

George Oberg

I lay numb to the pain
Opened my heart
For it was locked
A fortress under siege
But you I gave the key
Never knowing the assassin
Come in the night
A dagger thrust
Piercing my happiness
My hopes
My dreams
Dumbfounded Fingers laced I bleed
Through hands
Not meant to bind my own pain
Eviscerating my soul
Skillfully struck
The light in my eyes fading
Falling in love my sin
Both living and dead
Once again

Numb

Love Is...

Love is a fairytale we tell ourselves to chase away the shadows of loneliness.

What Cruelty

What cruelty
A heart so full of love
Defective
One made for breaking
I've always fallen for the kiss
The one who's intentions misplaced
The narcissist with an angels face.

About the Author

Caroline Derbes
@Caroline_creativecorner

Caroline Derbes discovered the joy of writing poetry at age 51, when a poetry professor, Sandford Lyne, taught her third-grade students how to use 4-word prompts that he called bait-buckets with which to catch a poem. She had taught for 29 years and spent the Covid lockdown typing long-closeted poems for her debut book, Poetic Self-Portrait. She and her husband have two children and 5 grandchildren.

*I've Got Pictures of You—
Someone I Used to Know*

Mental Prison

Our Love Poem

The Heart as a Diagram

His Garden

Intangible Emotion

Caroline Derbes

I've Got Pictures of You—
Someone I Used to Know

I thought your love would be a constant thing.
You used to adore me so,
saddled to my blue-jean, bell-bottomed hip,
not so long ago.

Nothing could have prepared me
for this yearning for the past.
Once brimming with lively,
admiration-filled companionship,
that bridge of dead logs
was burned—
not so long ago.

I will not let myself waste away
from the loss of your affection,
a kind of starvation,
an illness marked with a metallic taste.

Could a dog smell the schism
that brought this sad disease to me?
I search for that connection
in boxes of old photos—
smiles upon smiles,
taken not so long ago.

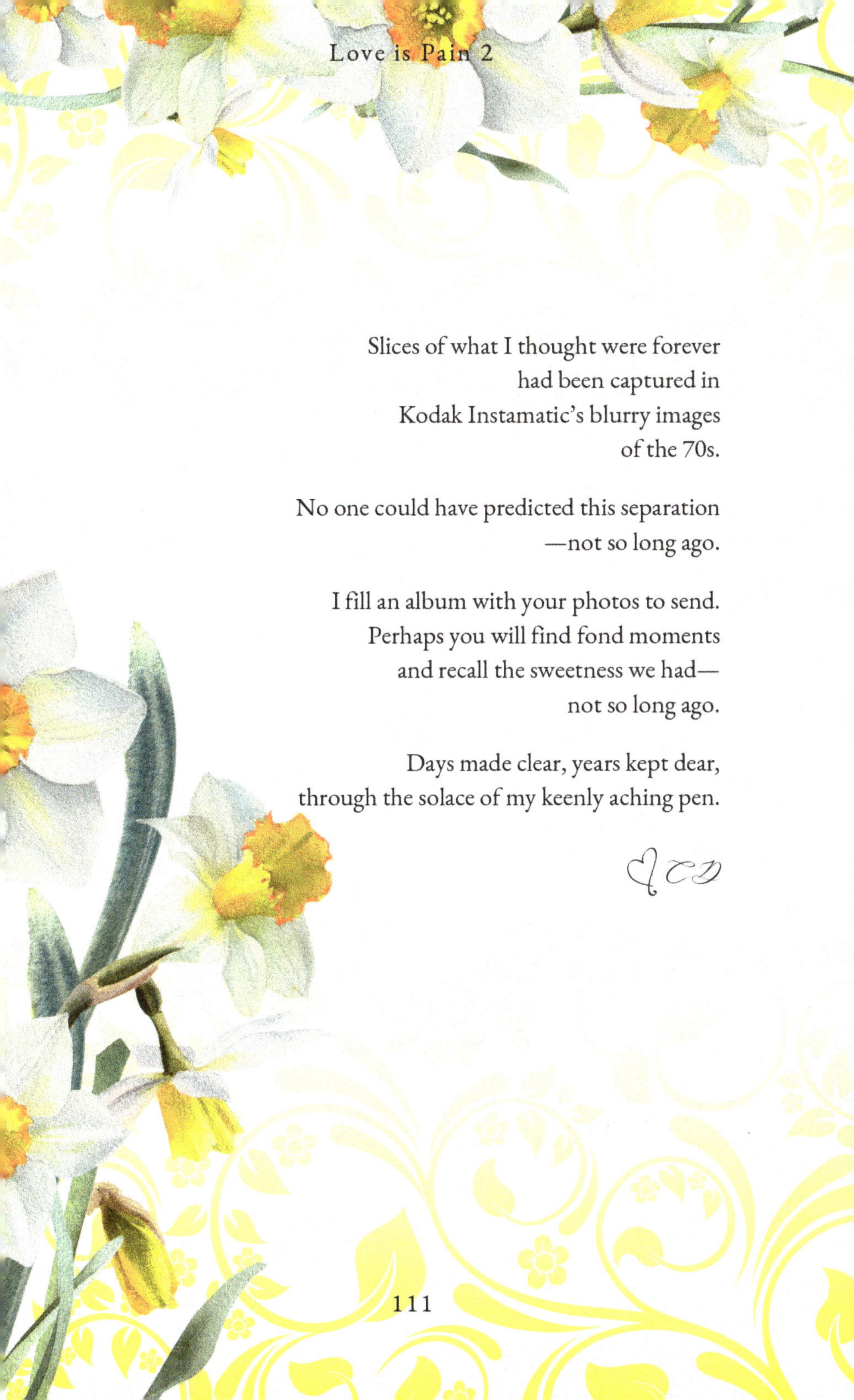

Slices of what I thought were forever
had been captured in
Kodak Instamatic's blurry images
of the 70s.

No one could have predicted this separation
—not so long ago.

I fill an album with your photos to send.
Perhaps you will find fond moments
and recall the sweetness we had—
not so long ago.

Days made clear, years kept dear,
through the solace of my keenly aching pen.

Caroline Derbes

Mental Prison

Overwhelming grief,
a mental prison,
nowhere to find relief.

Replaying that phone call,
wishing it had never been answered—
why did I not just stall?

Memories ricochet,
bouncing between skull walls,
replay after replay after replay.

My mind was reeling,
cloaked in depression,
a strange numbness of feeling.

Impervious to sound,
a sharp-shifting landscape—
my world turned around.

I tried writing him a letter:
"Dear Tom, don't be dead."
Truly cathartic, I did feel better.

My brain finally felt free,
memories now inked on paper—
haunting thoughts let me be.

Intangible emotion
permeated my being.
          Swallowed me whole.
First real impact.
          Stuck in Tears.
Quicksand's pull.

I became a specialist on the subject,
that year, of an unprepared for lesson.

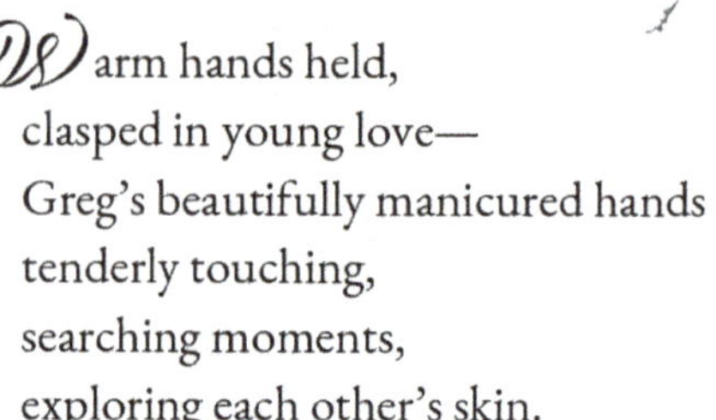

Caroline Derbes

*W*arm hands held,
clasped in young love—
Greg's beautifully manicured hands
tenderly touching,
searching moments,
exploring each other's skin.

Electrified sensations,
delicious awakenings.
In fifty years,
we've never neglected our passion,
sustained that gluing factor
with a little fiery imagination.
Our love poem continues.

My hands wrapped in his,
dancing in rhythmic warmth,
a collaboration of movements,
tuned to perfection.

Last year, an oldie on Muzak—
Johnny Rivers crooning.
He asked me to dance;
the empty restaurant beckoned.
The waitress exclaimed,
"Y'all are adorable!"

Our love poem is magic.

Our Love Poem

Hands that support each other,
demonstrated through caring tasks,
gestures of love—
preparing delicious dinners,
planting colorful gardens,
even mundane ones,
appreciated acts of love:
washing dishes,
changing sheets,
sweeping scrapes of daily living.

Though we've had our share
of disagreeable moments,
never a hand raised in anger.
Our love poem is patient.

Soothing tears,
consoling arms wrap me,
alleviating grief's trauma—
aftermath of Tom's suicide.

He said, "If I ever see that
expression on your face again,
I'll know that something
has happened to one of the children."

Our love poem succors.

continued

Caroline Derbes

Protective Papa Bear
flew to care for grown son, Clark,
in post-surgery concern.
No child of his would
go through that alone.

When Laura finally
decided to leave her X from hell,
Greg immediately paid the lawyer's fee—
cheaper than a murder sentence!

Our love poem defends.

Now in our 70s,
our love has entered a phase
of concern for aging bodies.
He worries about my falling again;
I tripped in the dark last night,
hitting my chin on a table.
I worry about his body's symptoms.

Our love poem cares.

When we bought this house,
I had never thought this tiny pool
would have such a bonding effect.

He's always made me laugh,
however, we've actually talked more
over pool-cocktails
than in the previous forty-five years.

Our love poem endures.

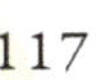

Caroline Derbes

The Heart as a Diagram

Landscape of My Heart.

Deep within my heart are signs
of a well-blazed trail—
step-step, step-step, step-step.

Layers of sediment have settled
into a lower cavern,
a thickening named
Ventricular Hypertrophy.

Along this path have been
long rivers, meandering wildly,
then forking in other directions.

In which direction should I paddle
my little canoe?

My heart has survived
boulders that have hit me in the face
as I have traveled turbulent white waters.

My heart speeds in desperate survival
at the crescendo of a pulling waterfall.

Sometimes, I slow down, observing leaves
as they peacefully float along beside me,
in awe of nature's wonders,
as I am carried through a quiet tributary.

Once I fell into a crevasse of grief.
My brother's suicide could have pulled me
into an eternal abyss of frozen tears.

However, my family, friends, and students
used sturdy ropes of vine
to pull me back to the surface
of that treacherous glacier.

With the suddenness of an earthquake,
a stroke shook my core and knocked me down.

I knew that no one could do
the recovery work for me.

Determined to get back on my feet,
I climbed, danced, Tai Chi'd, and Yoga'd
my way back with few residual effects.
Though my balance is a bit shaky,
a necessity on life's track.

A small Christmas concussion
made me feel as if I'd left the planet entirely.
My head, in another dimension,
was kept company by the constant humming
of fairies' wings.

Under the epicardium are foot-trails,
full of tripping hazards,
once wide, now narrowed,
with encroaching brush and branches—
sometimes slowing progress.

Peeking under fallen trees
grow mosses and lichens,
life's moments marking the surface
as would a carved monument.

Around the bend,
beautiful, distant mountain forests,
full of the unknown, still beckon
this adventurer to continue.

Caroline Derbes

His Garden

His loving hands come toward me,
planting carefully chosen seeds—
herbs: rosemary, dill, thyme, chives;
flowers: verbena, impatiens, day lilies,
tiara of zinnias, my crown.

Fertilizing the earth,
culling every weed with care,
watering me each morning,
pruning bushes annually,
protecting always,
sacrificing time, giving of himself,
creating his perfect garden.

While I, in turn, nourish him and his.
My tomato harvest provides
nutritious summer salads.
My herbs season delectable dishes.
My colorful blooms
provide beauty for yard and home,
offering a peaceful sanctuary.

Yet, I cannot provide
the Eden he or she imagined.
Floating in her pool,
behind her sunglasses—hidden tears.

Not refreshing enough
for her tortured, alcoholic soul—
my beauty, the pool's cool waters
in his garden.

Only a temporary safe haven
from his acerbic tones,
his foul mouth,
his drunken cruelty.

I witness her lonely sojourns,
her desperate searches—
finding his supposedly hidden beers.

Not nearly far enough
from her demanding need.

Why does he continue
creating temptation for her?
He knows
she is not strong enough
to resist the luring call.

Intoxicated by liquor—
not by love,
voices waft out to me,
voices of anger, recrimination, regret,
unlike the soft, soothing sounds he
hums to me,
his cherished garden.

continued

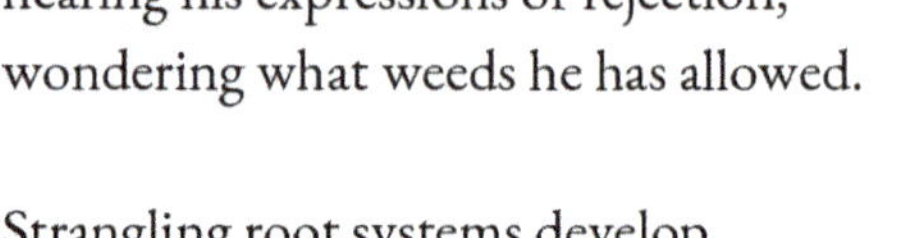

Caroline Derbes

I observe and wonder,
watching him planting seeds of discontent,
seeing his lack of affection,
hearing his expressions of rejection,
wondering what weeds he has allowed.

Strangling root systems develop,
weakening his relationships daily.

Killing his wife,
under his scorching words, she wilts.
She is dying
like an untended garden.

My gardener,
worshipping nature, nurturing me,
while, at the same time,
destroying the sanctity of their marriage,
neglecting to protect,
caring not for the sacred covenant.

Observing him tenderly caring
for my plants each day,
I cannot help but wonder—
what would their lives be,
what would grow,
if he nurtured his relationships
with the same loving attention,
the same tender touch,
the same devotion that he does me, his garden?

For Betsy
♡ CD

About the Author

Kheneil Black

This Jamaican Born, Canadian poet is a proud father and husband. Founder & Co-Host of Musiac Mondays and Co-founder of The 6ix Poets Society, he enjoys writing, spending time with his family and many other creative writing endeavors and most things from the nerdosphere, including but not limited to comics, video games, anime and movies. He loves to foster growth and encourage poets to explore other writing avenues and never stop writing.

"The world is too small to make enemies" -Kheneil Black

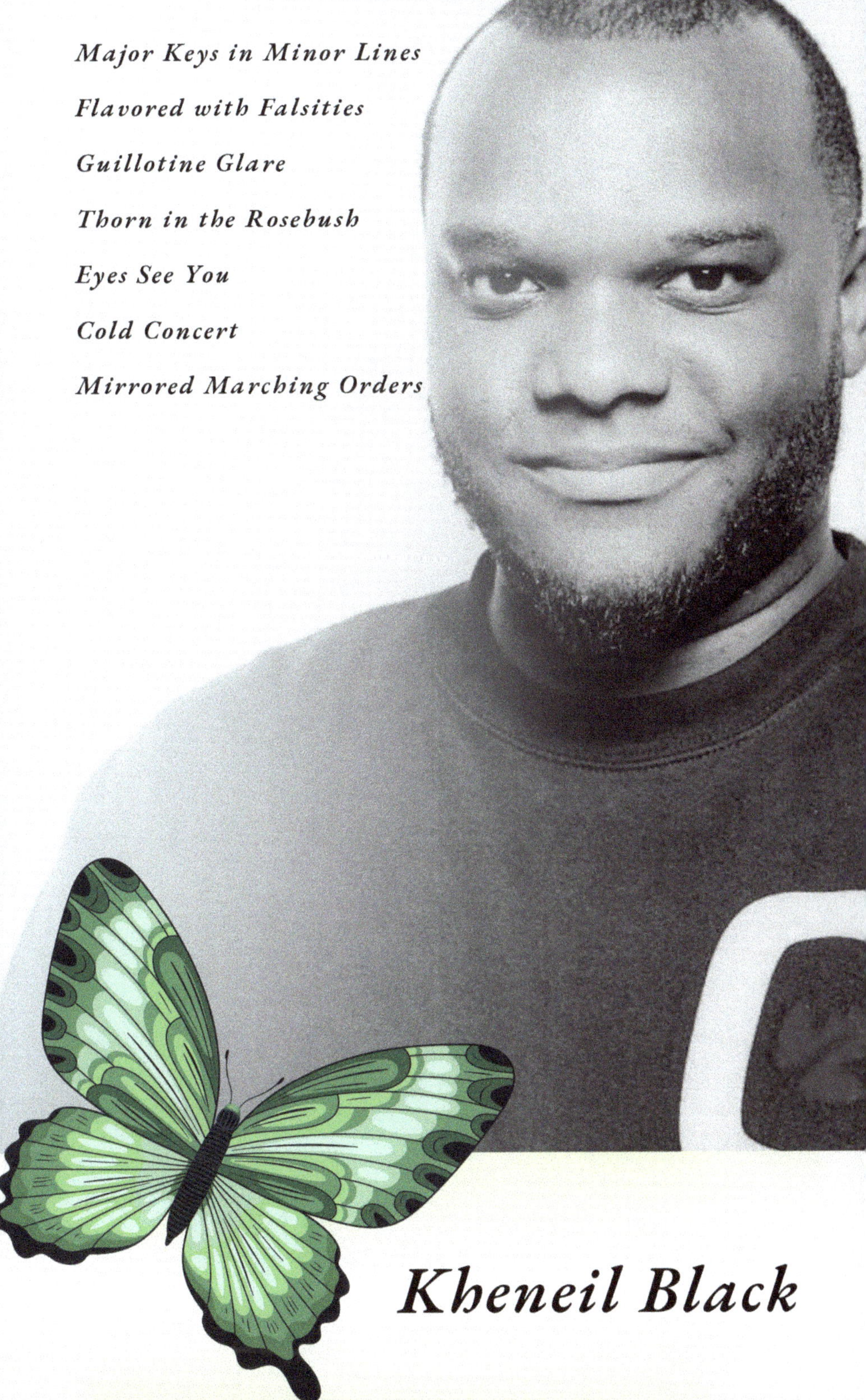

Major Keys in Minor Lines
Flavored with Falsities
Guillotine Glare
Thorn in the Rosebush
Eyes See You
Cold Concert
Mirrored Marching Orders
Kheneil Black

The Parasite of reality is the truth in the depths of trauma.

Private moments of acceptance are the footprints to healing.

Forgiveness is the voice that nests in growth.

Consumption of guilt will build a vault of self loathing.

Pools of reflection can quench your thirst for self love.

Bathe in your own brilliance and wash your pain away.

KB

Major Keys in Minor Lines

Betrayal is a hell of a dish,
with fonted lies as the garnish.
Served coldly in bold,
perhaps in ALL CAPS,
cups full to the brim.
Underlining the underlying truth.
Words with incriminating italics,
leaning under the pressures
in lieu of better decisions.
Blindsided by food for thought
laced with maggots of deceit.
Bon Appetit.

♡ JKB

Flavored With Falsities

Kheneil Black

Guillotine Glare

If looks could kill...

That stare you indelibly share is razor-sharp.
I'm in visual range of the serrated ocular blades.
Your malicious side-eye is used
to pare my thinning skin off, untamed.

I turned my face because you could maim a guy
with your chainsaws for eyes.
That frozen steel in your pupils
telegraphs my plight.
I don't know how to proceed as you scream,

"Get out of my sight!"

I'm clearly unaware of my folly,
pre-loaded apologies cut down before being uttered.

The Ginsu dance will ensue soon.
My mind's eye flies through my actions of the day,
hoping that a moment of silence would whisk the tension away.

My awareness is naked on the cold stone chopping block,
and my world trembles in fear of being rocked.

Your glare, diamond-coated,
the guillotine of disdain
locked in and ready to drop.

I wished the night sky wasn't so starry.
I have yet to know why,
but I'll be sorry....

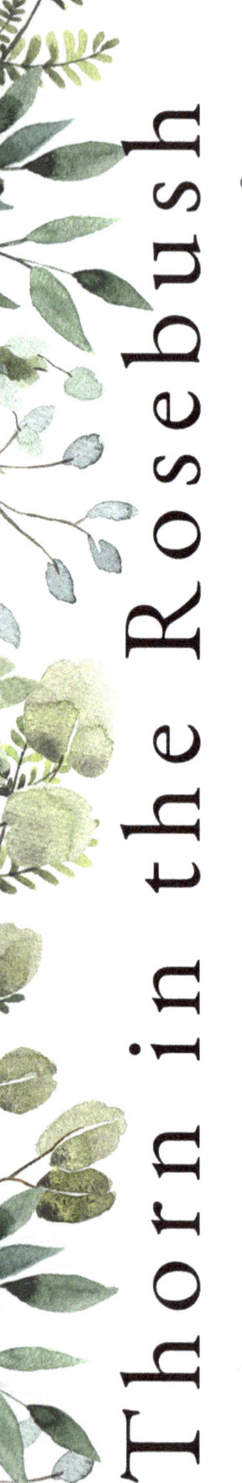

Kheneil Black

$\mathcal{A}$ fluttering of rose aroma
cascades around lovers,
beneath a sycamore veil.

The Moon lassos fog
atop a crabgrass floor.

The rhythmic murmurs
of froggie falsetto float aloft the silence.
A space free of killed joys
erects a stage devoid of restraint.

Nothing like a gentle ravishing,
 escalating into a tangent
of applauding hips
to open the ventricles.
Tandem-clasped lips,
wrestling closer—
lip-locked as it were.

Poised for insertion,
the twain releases
their barricade of passions,
kept at bay
by a gaunt patience.

Yearning grows cavalier
in the face of unbridled tender touches.

Skin to skin,
with the intention to cream within—
derma gluttens a proximitous sin.

Love is Pain 2

Two bodies purchase pleasurable pains;
thorns in the rose bush
serve both to gain.

Dew drops from tantric activities
soak the surroundings,
matching the intentions of the evening.

Thighs, hands, and fingers intertwine,
grappling for oneness.

The wilderness of heartbeats
serves the best battleground
for the calamity of pounding and pumping,
befitting an industrial-strength humping.

Sweat sizzles on dermis
from nose to navel,
in concert with bodily shivers.

In a completed heap,
they are satiated—
with the mutual comings and goings,
movings and groovings,
quiverings and oozings
achieved during their night together.

Bated breath beckons
for a second round:
a sound pounding,
a nocturnal nearness.

131

Eyes See You

Kheneil Black

You bombarded my pupils.

You've burnt your beauty marks into my POV.
The silhouette of your valleys and dips can't be
unseen by my now-naked eyes.
You have built a home inside my eyelids.

My cornea bends your light into my heart
and decorates my thoughts.

Your measurements have been 3d printed in my
daily dreams.

I can see you clearly as you stare into me.

My darkness is repulsed by my view of you.

Being blinded by your beauty
has given me ultimate clarity.

Watch me watching you as I feed your image to
my hungry retinas. Your face and all your other
places are on the menu.

You are more than food for thought.
You are a buffet made just for me. I'll open my
eyes wide and swallow you whole.

Her feminine falsetto reverberated as she left,
placing glaciers of regret
on my now sharp ivory skeleton
before the notes were ever played.

A concerto of chill meanders
across my shivering skin,
tuning my thoughts to match
the vibrations of freezing ache.

Terrifying scales of loneliness
crescendo upon my bones.
Spine-chilling pains become the metronome
to the beat of my wintered heart.

The subzero memories
strike chords of panic,
riding a baritone moan
to the slippery floor of my efforts.

Her icy piano plays a melody
too hot to handle
and too cold to hold.

So I remain bold
and choose to focus on myself,
with my fingers placed on the right keys.

I just want someone to warm me up.
I'm not looking for Treble.

KB

Cold Concert

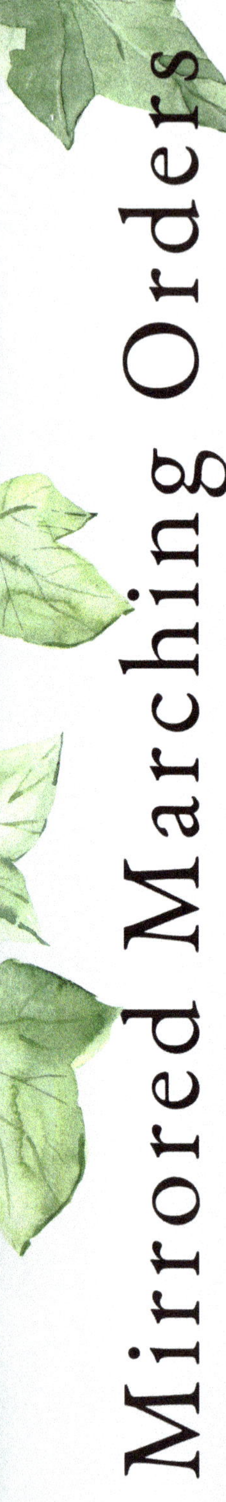

Mirrored Marching Orders

Kheneil Black

*O*nward I march—
my wildest dreams form the vanguard of promises,
combating naysayers,
for fruition's sake.

In reverse, I adjust,
spinning on heel,
I reveal the Achilles' doom to my aforementioned plans.
I shift the weight of resistance,
pivoting the negative energies away
from my intended path,
 clearing the way for progression.

To the right, I strafe—
the unbridled lies hurled in my general direction
by the digital vomit conglomerates.

To the left I leap—
flying over those who chose to operate
on low-lying tactics and unaligned frequencies.
I never beg them, not even to differ.

I demand to differ,
and defer any thoughts
that would suggest otherwise
to what I have to declare next.

Every inhale received
is for the purpose of advancement
of the exhale preceding it.

To think otherwise is a white flag
to the demons that chase you,
a declaration of defeat
to the darkness.

Cracks in your brooding intentions
don't need a seven-year assignment.

The night lives its zenith
just before it's shattered by the day.

I will be my own lighthouse
off the coast of Frenemy Bay.

We all have the strength
to rescue ourselves
from our own reflections.

KB

About the Author

Elizabeth O. Ogunmodede

Elizabeth O. Ogunmodede is widely recognized as Nigeria's youngest media mogul, making remarkable strides in the industry at just 17 years old. As an accomplished author, entrepreneur, and creative visionary, Elizabeth began her writing journey at the age of 8. By 16, she had already ascended to the role of CEO at Eye Opener Productions Global Network Ltd., a flourishing media company she founded. With six published books to her name, Elizabeth exemplifies multifaceted talent. She is not only a publisher but also excels as a product designer, graphic designer, book cover designer, book trailer producer, spoken word artist, and website developer. Among her literary projects, her most ambitious is an Afrofantasy novel titled Halloween in Africa, which showcases her unique storytelling and cultural creativity.

Her passion project, Author Lifestyle and Book Talk Magazine, is a quarterly international publication that celebrates literature, art, and the author lifestyle. It has earned acclaim in the United States and beyond, serving as a testament to her relentless drive and innovative spirit.

Presently, Elizabeth is combining her literary creativity with her passion for law by developing a vital initiative aimed at bridging the gap between the public and credible legal practitioners. Recognizing that the human world is governed by laws and that ignorance of the law is no excuse, she is dedicated to building a seamless connection that brings trusted legal expertise closer to people—effortlessly and without stress. This mission embodies her utmost goal and vision: to create a vital legal support platform that enhances access to justice. As a teenage entrepreneur and visionary, Elizabeth Ogunmodede is living proof that age is no barrier to success. Fueled by passion, creativity, and unwavering determination, she is on a mission to inspire, empower, and make a lasting impact on the world.

Elizabeth O. Ogunmodede

The Delicacy Called Love

According to your wishes,
I could whip up mouthwatering dishes
and serve you treats,
made with my special recipes.

In my teenage days,
I'd mastered the culinary art
with all my heart,
and now, I've charmed many hearts.

I am a master of the kitchen art,
with many feathers to my hat.
I learned there was a delicacy,
and it became my fantasy
to search every cookbook,
to find every chef in the loop
of this trend that kept me hooked.

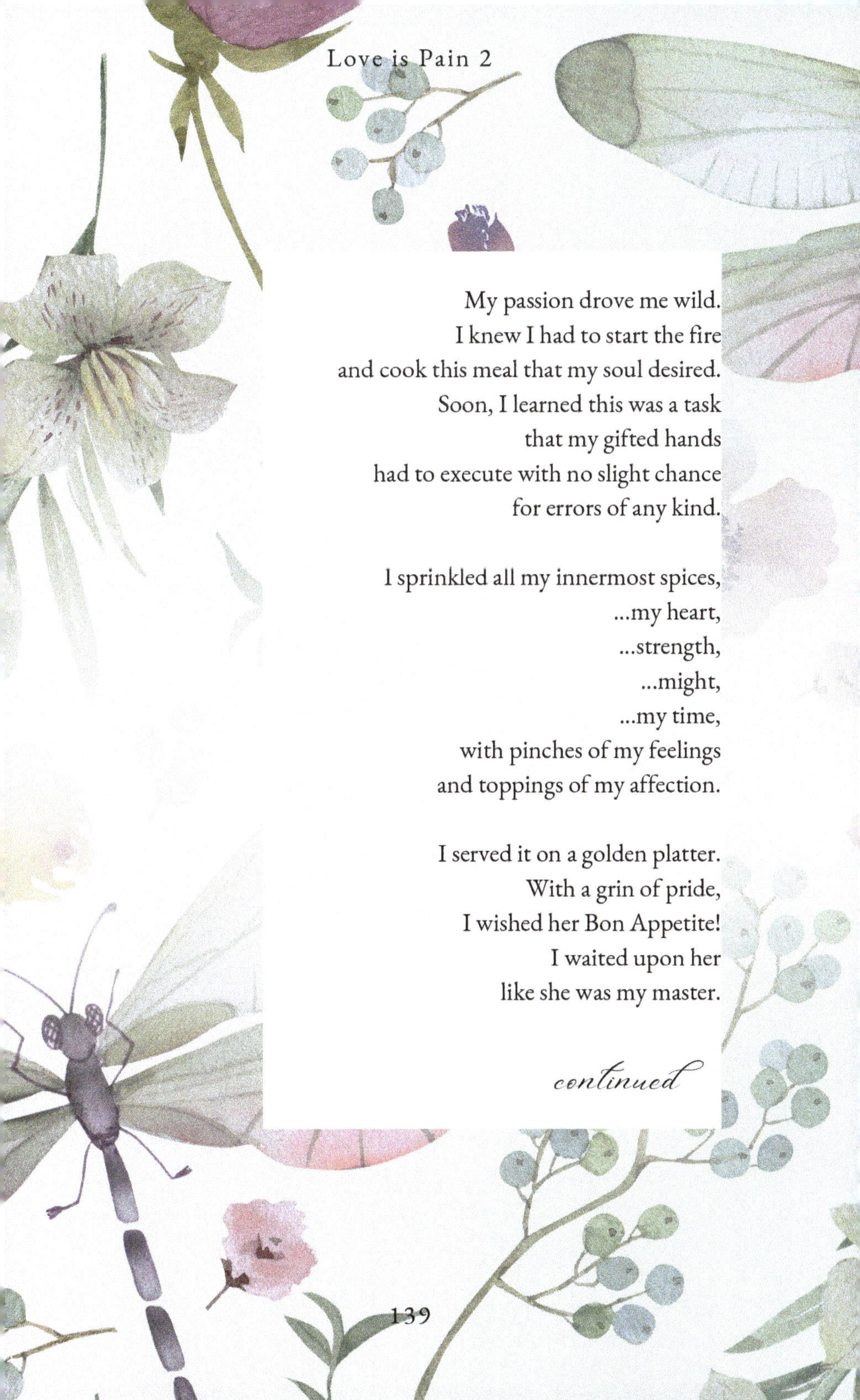

My passion drove me wild.
I knew I had to start the fire
and cook this meal that my soul desired.
Soon, I learned this was a task
that my gifted hands
had to execute with no slight chance
for errors of any kind.

I sprinkled all my innermost spices,
...my heart,
...strength,
...might,
...my time,
with pinches of my feelings
and toppings of my affection.

I served it on a golden platter.
With a grin of pride,
I wished her Bon Appetite!
I waited upon her
like she was my master.

continued

She trashed my feelings
and hard work
into bin with no rethink.
Shredded my heart
without batting an eye.
She scraped my strength off the plate
and my might could put up no fight.

Fountain of tears
poured down from my eyes
like a waterfall from a fantasy world.
I thought I'd drown in my sorrows,
thought pain would wrench my heart
like no tomorrow,
but I'd lost the key to my feelings,
...the passion that drove me strongly
and the power that kept me standing.

Alas! I was wrong.
I should never have thought
that the delicacy called love
was a sweet dish that gave joy.

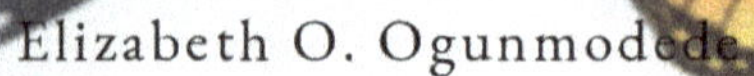

Elizabeth O. Ogunmodede

I Got Lost In The Fantasy

At twilight,
we stood at the Eiffel Tower.
I found comfort in your arms,
joy in your free spirit
that eased my mind.
"Your smile lights up the dark",
was the sound of your whisper.

Winter came,
furious storms and snowfall,
frost-covered ground, and frostbite.
While grey clouds and mist
kept us company through the day,
you held my gloved hands tight.
With a wide grin, you said,
"You are my sunshine".

Every hour of the day,
you kept me happy
I found comfort in your embrace
...in the scent of your musky cologne
and the sound of your melodic baritone
When you smiled at me,
I felt my insides get mushy,
a furious blush coloring my face.

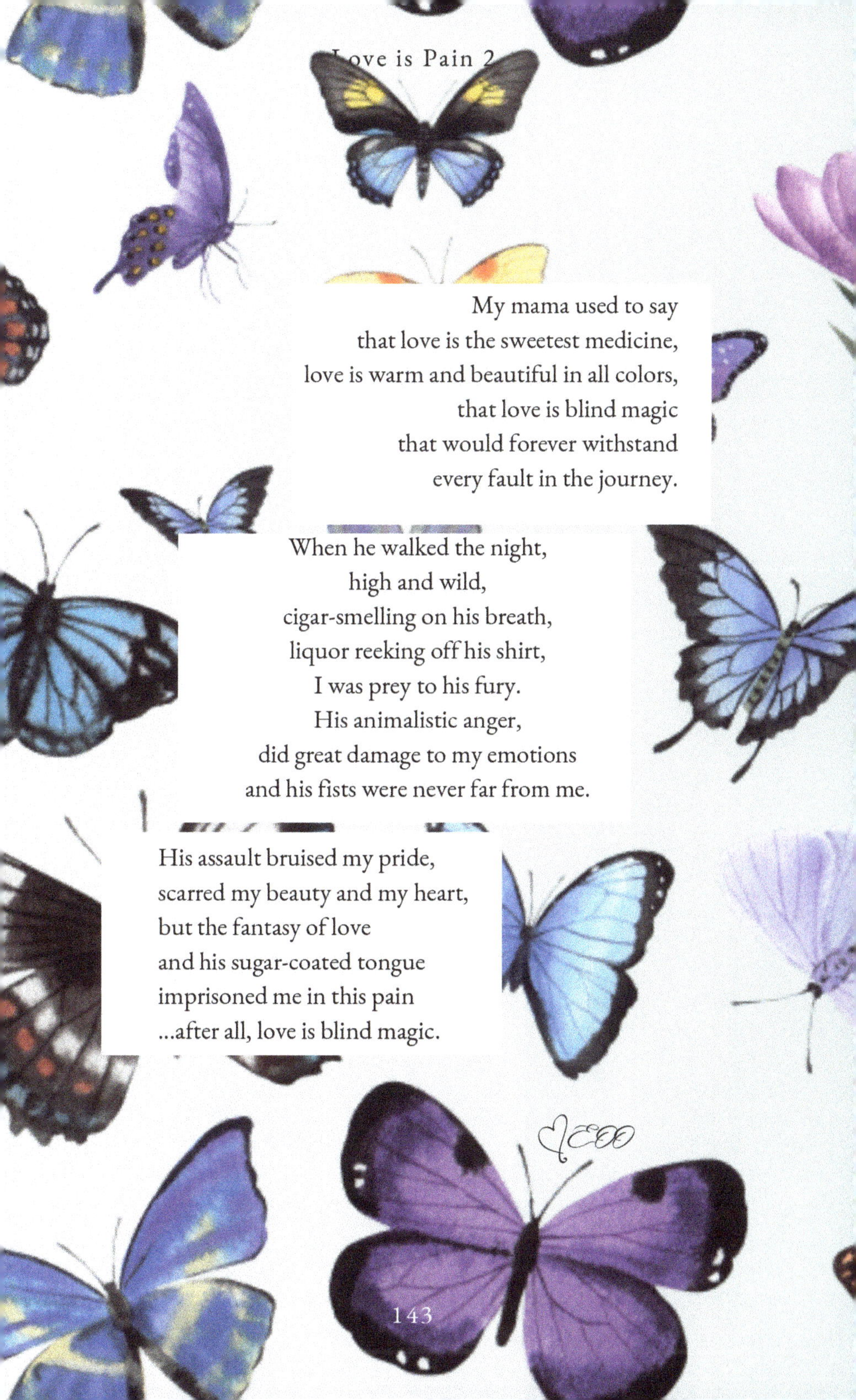

My mama used to say
that love is the sweetest medicine,
love is warm and beautiful in all colors,
that love is blind magic
that would forever withstand
every fault in the journey.

When he walked the night,
high and wild,
cigar-smelling on his breath,
liquor reeking off his shirt,
I was prey to his fury.
His animalistic anger,
did great damage to my emotions
and his fists were never far from me.

His assault bruised my pride,
scarred my beauty and my heart,
but the fantasy of love
and his sugar-coated tongue
imprisoned me in this pain
...after all, love is blind magic.

Elizabeth O. Ogunmodede

How The Pains Grew

I come from a special world,
a place where our colors
charms the mind and our scents
holds strong, alluring spirits,
that attracts the nostrils.

I come from a regal family,
my color is a dazzling red,
the kind that is appreciated
when love and romance steal the air.

Valentine came flying in,
I was offered to a pretty lady
in a fancy restaurant.
She sniffed my petals,
with joyful laughter
and adoring gaze.

I could feel the love in the air,
see the woman's blush.
I could almost feel the butterflies
erupting in her stomach
from all the sweet moments spent
with the charming man.

She welcomed me to her house,
putting me in a vase.
I was starting to feel my vigor
rubbing off of me.
I could feel my petals
lose their attractive sheen.

I had always known
that death was never far off
in our beautiful world.
But never thought
I'd miss mother Earth soon.

continued

Elizabeth O. Ogunmodede

I was birthed
with charms of love and romance,
eager to please and spread love.
But as the cool evening sprang on me,
gently playing with my withering petals,
I feel a longing for love,
I feel a desire to be caressed,
to be returned to Mother Earth,
to live one more life.

Oh! My excitement died
and my pains grew
as she lounged with him
on the couch,
watching movies and
listening to music.
I was forgotten,
my moment of glory
was long gone past
and all that is left
is a realization that love
did not speak for me.

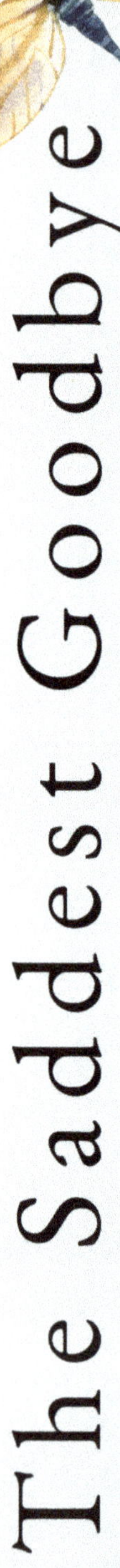

The Saddest Goodbye

Elizabeth O. Ogunmodede

That day on the ice rink,
when you fell on your knees,
I knew I was whipped.

As I lifted you back on your feet,
your gorgeous smile
made everything a blur.
You became my only focus,
and as the days went by,
I fell deeper in love
with no wish to let you go.

Our worlds were meant
to lie apart,
our dreams flew high
in different directions.

Yet, I willed myself
to hold onto the fantasy of your love,
but reality pulled us apart.

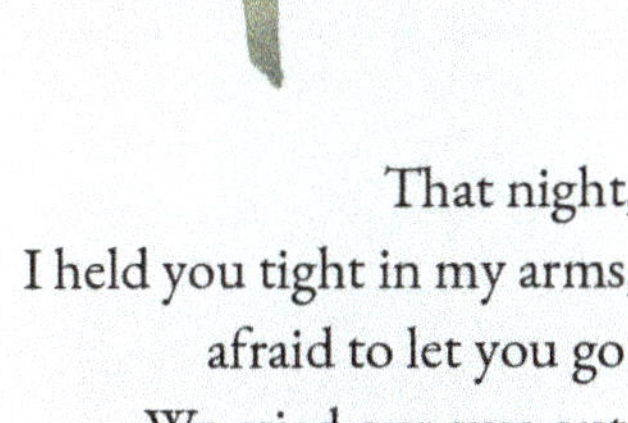

That night,
I held you tight in my arms,
afraid to let you go.
We cried our eyes out.

I whispered goodbye in your ears,
and you wiped my tears,
planting kisses on my face.

We spent the night recalling memories
that would carry us through the years.
And when I caressed your face,
I printed the picture of your beauty
in my mind,
never to be forgotten.

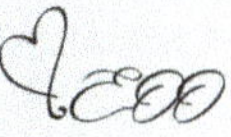

Elizabeth O. Ogunmodede

The Perfect Moment

It was her dream
to walk on the clouds of love,
to be high and drunk on love potion,
to find love in the arms of a dashing man
who would dance with her
in the rain of his affection
like the romcoms that she loved to see.

Every man that crossed her path
seemed to be her perfect match.
Her young age and innocence
were no match
for the brutality of the world.

Her heart was too tender
to bear the pain of love,
yet she wanted nothing more
than a taste of sweet love.

The days went by,
taking along the innocent film
which coated her heart.

The hands of love
were not the softest.
They manhandled her
and dyed her heart black
in pure hatred for every man
that ever crossed her path,
and a huge regret:
If only I'd waited for the perfect moment.

It Isn't Right

I never wish to fall in love again,
if the route to take
has no lights to brighten my path.

I never wish to fall in love again,
if the wind on this journey
blows my senses away.

I never wish to fall in love again,
if you will never hear my cry
...never give heed to my voice.

I never wish to fall in love again,
if the blindfold of love
will be bound upon my eyes.

Because when I walked,
I couldn't see the roads.
Every injury and fall
weakened my bravado
and my belief in love.
So, I wished for just one thing:
that *love isn't blind.*

Elizabeth O. Ogunmodede

I've Shut My Door

I can hear your knocks,
...can hear you calling,
but I'd made my choice
before you came along.

I was jilted,
my tired heart was pained,
suffering from heartbreak,
no one could heal me.

My life was in shambles,
when he came along
with claim to save me,
my hope surfaced highly.

He charmed my heart
and our bond grew strong.
His steadfast cheer
saw me to the finish line,
where he deserted me
when all was to be fine.

Yet again,

my heart shattered
in multiple pieces
~non-glueable~

I walked down the beach,
at night's cool hour
with a broken heart
~locked up~

With a deep sigh,
I chucked the key down the sea,
burying all my grief.
As the cold rippled through my skin,
I felt my heart harden
and door closed shut.

Elizabeth O. Ogunmodede

How It Withered

I loved to see flowers in bloom,
I longed for my birth season,
when all would come alive,
erupting with a burst of life.

I loved to hold pretty flowers,
with appealing hues,
that catches the eye.
I used to think,
that our love was vibrant
like these flowers.

What we shared was colorful,
a fruitful bond,
attracting many people,
we had it all.

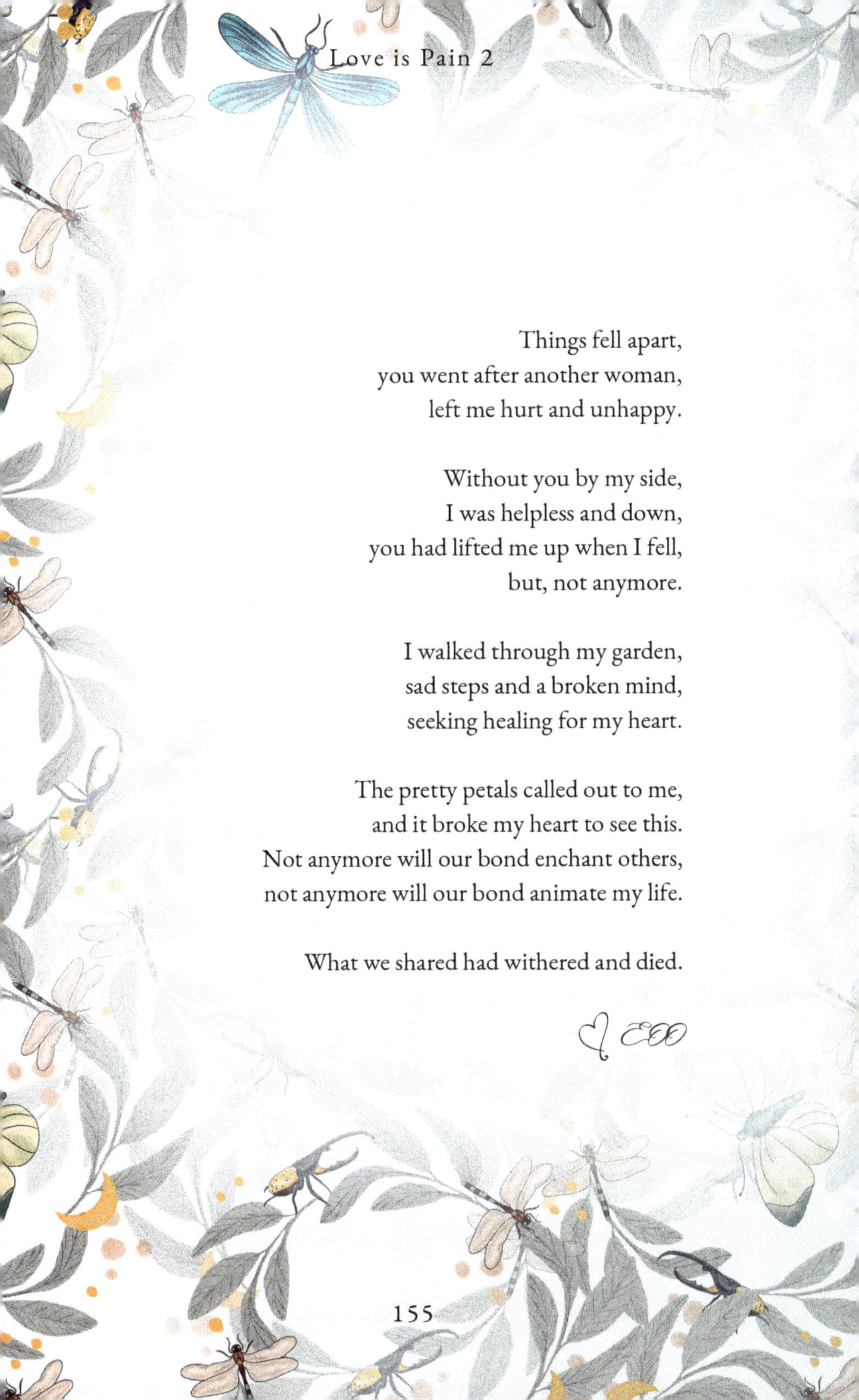

Things fell apart,
you went after another woman,
left me hurt and unhappy.

Without you by my side,
I was helpless and down,
you had lifted me up when I fell,
but, not anymore.

I walked through my garden,
sad steps and a broken mind,
seeking healing for my heart.

The pretty petals called out to me,
and it broke my heart to see this.
Not anymore will our bond enchant others,
not anymore will our bond animate my life.

What we shared had withered and died.

Elizabeth O. Ogunmodede

Too Young To Love

My tender heart
was too feeble
for the punches of love—
hard blows that broke my jaw,
rendering me speechless.

My mind was too soft,
and my brains
too young to know right from wrong.

I was infatuated with love,
carried away by the sweet words
and gorgeous paintings of love,
but when it struck me hard
with pain and heartbreak,
my young heart shattered,
and my innocence became tainted.

Faded Footprints

Dusty feet,
shuffling through bushes,
leading to the golden sands
where he lay,
in a dried pool of blood,
eyes open wide in terror,
deep gashes on his fair skin.

The spotless white of his suit
now colored in the deep red
of his blood—
~a picture of disgust~
that distorts her bowels.

...She throws up
with tears in her eyes.
Unable to bear this pain
in her heart,
her legs give way,
and her eyes flutter
in submission to dizziness.

She falls to the ground,
her white bridal garment
kisses the sands,
and everything turns black.

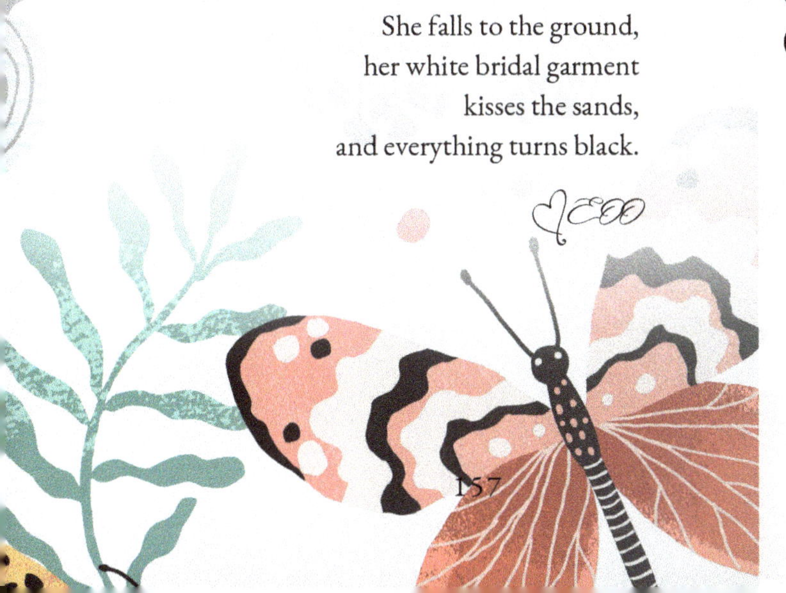

Elizabeth O, Ogunmodede

Wish The Rain Could Wash My Tears

*E*ach day stirs the memory
of that woeful night
that tore me apart.

The wheels that drive my way
threaten to send me back
to that very hour
when my joy ended.

Each time I walk the roads,
my spirit turns dead.
My heart pounds endlessly
from deep pain within my soul,
regret burns my mind.

If I could turn the hands of time,
I would never have boozed
my throat,
would never have driven them home
when the spirit of alcohol
controlled my vision.

I linger on my steps,
deliberately soaking in the rain,
wishing the rain could wipe my tears
and wash the guilt from my soul—
...the deep pain of losing my loved ones.

Can someone hear my cry?

The agony in my heart
that my voice lets out?
The torment that I bear
in the torturous hands of love
drives me crazy
...distorts my inner peace.

This chain that binds me,
restrains my joy,
leaves me starving,
and craving freedom.
Can someone set me free
from the torturous hands of love?

I Crave For Freedom

About
the
Author

Daphne Lane

Daphne Lane is a red-haired, spunky, eighteen-year-old high school student who started writing poetry in 2023. She is a brilliant artist who loves to paint, crochet, knit, craft, and pretty much just create beautiful things. She is interested in Criminal Justice and possibly becoming a PI someday. She also has shown interest in interior and graphic design. Daphne loves animals and making TikTok videos. She also has an affinity for Takis and Monster drinks. This is her very first publication. If you care to reach her, write the publisher at where.beautiful.inks@gmail.com

Say it to Your Face

You

No More

Video Game

I Wonder

At Fault

Yet

Daphne Lane

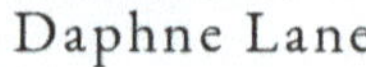

Daphne Lane

"*I* don't want you talking to other girls."
But I don't say that to your face.
"I don't want you following other girls."
But again, I don't say that to your face.

"I want your location."
"I want updates about your whereabouts and
what you're doing."
"I want flowers and to be posted by you."
But again, again, and again, I do not say that to
your face.

I overthink.
I get jealous.
I want you to myself.
But I don't want that control.
I want it on its own.
I want it from you cause you want it to.
Not because I want you to.
Yet again, I'll never say that to your face.

Say it to Your Face

The fear built up, yet the anger settled in.
The overthinking, yet the jealousy.
The self heartbreak, yet the love for you.
The trust.
Yet the emptiness left once you'll have gone.

Something I'll never quite get...
I expect the least.
Yet you have presented the most.
Thus, why I don't say it to your face.

♡DL

Daphne Lane

You were everything
my father could never amount to.
You gave me everything
a father should have taught me to look for.
Instead of searching, you came to me.
But I didn't really know how to treat you.
So instead, I lost you.
And that's on me.
not...
YOU.

164

No More

And that was it.
No more "I love you".
No more "When can we hang next?"
No more "Nooo I win".
No more kisses.
No more hugs.
Was it all just a dream?
Were you ever even real?
Yesterday you were mine...
But today we aren't fine.
You are my sweet boy.
Where did I go wrong?
We were everything but now...
No more.

Life's like a video game.
We all spawn in and fight to survive.
We make friends,
We laugh a little.
But one day... those people will never
come back.
They'll vanish.
Start a family with someone, and you'll
be forgotten.
That's just the way life works.

♡DL

I wonder if he ever thinks,
"Wow, she's beautiful."
I wonder if he ever tells his friends
"She's so amazing."
I wonder if he tells his parents
"This girl is perfect."
I wonder if he ever stares and admires me
I wonder if I'm ever the last thought on his mind
before he goes to sleep
Because although I may not be this...
"Perfect, ideal girl,"
I still love him like he's the only boy in the world.

♡ *DL*

I Wonder

Daphne Lane

Am I at fault for getting attached?
Or is it him for letting me?
Am I at fault for being forgiving?
Or is it him for letting me?
I sit and wonder what went wrong.
But then, I put myself at fault.
I am at fault for caring so much.
I am at fault for getting attached.
I am at fault for letting it slide.
But am I?
We were fine, then it all just crumbled.
Where did I go wrong?
Was my love not strong enough...?

At Fault

Your lips say you love me...
Yet your actions say otherwise.
It's girl after girl...
Yet for me, it's block after block.
I try my best to make you comfortable...
Yet you don't reciprocate.
Again and again, I ask for this closure...
Yet you get upset when I ask.
I get that you try.
I get that you understand.
I get that you care.
Yet, you haven't proven that.

About the Author

Diane Lipton Gollub

Diane Lipton Gollub is an attorney, artist, musician, poet, and philanthropist residing in New York. A graduate of Brandeis University in Waltham, Massachusetts, she earned Cum Laude degrees in Sociology/Criminology and Fine Arts in 1977. She then went on to study at The School of Visual Arts in Manhattan, creating portfolios in Graphic Design, Advertising, and Package Design. She began her career as the Art Director for Sasson Jeans, Inc. in New York City in 1978, at 21.

After marriage in 1979, Diane commenced the study of law at St. John's University School of Law in New York. Upon passing the bar exam, she commenced her legal career at The Office of the District Attorney in Nassau County, New York. Her philanthropic activities include work at Island Harvest, a food rescue charity that supplies food throughout Long Island, New York, becoming the Vice President of Community Relations at Child Abuse Prevention Services in New York, where she voluntarily taught Child Abuse Law in high schools on Long Island, and to Mandated Reporters. Also serving on the Board of Directors of The Rosa Lee Young Childhood Center in Rockville Centre, New York. Chosen to be amongst those selected to review a study of all public schools in Rockville Centre, determining what funds were needed for their improvement.

The proud mother of Hayley Meredith Gollub and Ross Brandon Gollub, Diane was widowed in 2004, losing her beloved husband of 25 years. She became involved in Instagram in 2019 through her daughter's suggestion as a means to lift her perpetual sense of loss and the grief felt within widowhood. Her poetry evolved after being embraced by the loving community of artists within Instagram. She remains forever grateful to all who have inspired her to feel that her voice should be heard.

Diane Lipton Gollub

Diane Lipton Gollub

My Darling,

Tell me from your perspective, way up high;
how do you fall asleep
with the light of the moon in your eyes?
Have you become privy
to that place, flowers go
the moment they die?

Has it been revealed to you;
what sources those tears
that fill up the clouds?
Does Cumulus converse with Nimbostratus
when deciding upon whom
their bounty to enshroud?

Does your view from behind the stars
now enable you to see, what will befall all—
exactly who shall suffer calamity?

Tell me, Beloved, whatever is the point
of those feeble attempts made
in chasing our yesterdays?
Inner peace, never again to be found
in those same sacred ways
in which we were once blessed to have lovingly swayed.

Please do me the service of revealing to me,
perhaps within my dreams,
why life will never again
be exactly as it once seemed.

Diane Lipton Gollub

Within Serendipity's Clandestine Dance With Destiny

We humans, mere peons
within a cosmos, divine,
too many neglect to credit
the power that lies in the sky.

To the sun, the moon,
the stars, too few relate,
for we each emerge
within one precise moment of time—
receiving a destined fate.

Within serendipity's clandestine dance with destiny,
we are each bestowed our unique chemistry.

If two should meet,

remain out of sync,

learn to acknowledge

that this match

is not what you think.

For we are granted finite years upon this Earth, so sublime,
do not waste them mourning those loves lost,
for a truer love shall perhaps emerge—
after rolling the dice that you toss.

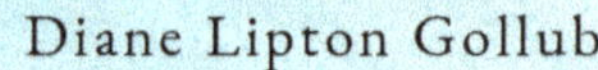

Diane Lipton Gollub

Locked within a labyrinth of life,
all paths chosen,
resulting in strife.

No matter which way I turn,
destined destruction earned,
I learn as I burn.

Spectators view this distance
I am relegated to roam,
floors leading nowhere,
much like this poem.

No way to get out,
I persistently shout,
there's no door in this hall,
reach an end,
there's a wall!

Trapped in a maze,
I remain dazed,
eternal, infernal existence—cuts like a knife,
such are my years
in the labyrinth of life.

Labyrinth of Life

The Winds of Chaotic Catastrophe

Swept up in the winds
of chaotic catastrophe,
each day a new battle forged
to maintain any semblance of sanity.

This sojourn uphill, continuous—
no specific destination within sight,
blackened ash blinding me
as I fiercely forge forward with all of my might.

Beware,

Father Time continuously ticking,
seemingly quicker than the beat of my heart;
feeling inundated by the weight of futility,
watching a world proceeding to fall apart.

Beyond The Clouds

Diane Lipton Gollub

I bid thee to look beyond the composition
of those heavy clouds that appear to unleash gloom,
for they have become saturated with tears of misery,
resulting from pervasive doom.

Beware, as the Earth continues its revolution,
ever circuitous,
consequences shall be duly unleashed,
those that karma has deemed fortuitous.

Behold, beyond these clouds,
the sun continues to shine,
imparting sustenance for growth,
sourced from somewhere Divine.

While in the midst of those catastrophes
unyielding, descending,
'tis taxing to seize onto a ray of light,
unbending.

Amidst those tragedies
which currently abound,
it becomes necessary to broaden perspective,
what was up, is now down.

Promise can be found in hope
that goodness shall overcome evil,
those responsible for unleashing such sorrow will find
their eternal residence lies with the Devil.

Love is Pain 2

So surreptitiously you swerved,
sashaying sleekly into my soul,
stepping up with increasing frequency,
those maniacal methods to seize all control!
Dismissive of decisions decidedly determined by me,
within a tenuous trance, I succumbed to your omnipotence,
too willingly.

Virtual veils of varying intensity, released
to intentionally obscure my existing identity.
With the prowess of a puppet master,
you proceeded to pluck the strings of my persona,
bizarrely going as far as to pick my perfume,
a most cloying aroma.

The veritable vanity ventured by you,
its volume, invariably vacuous,
you persist on an endless quest to fill it,
each attempt, disastrous!

Appropriating the lifeblood of others
whose radiance you deem more conspicuous.
I have now awakened to the reality which I can lucidly see,
loving you will, invariably, be the end of me!

The 'me' you initially saw is now one no one can see,
I hasten to extract myself from the tentacles
of your *deserv-ed* misery!

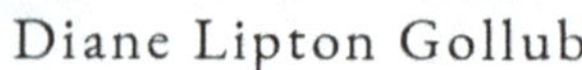
Diane Lipton Gollub

These Fathomless Depths

These fathomless depths
into which sensitive souls become drenched
when struck by sorrow too searing
to ever make sense,
for inexplicable reasons, from pure happiness—
I became wrenched.

How vivid remains that day, years ago,
we pledged our devotion,
in eyes so young,
brimming—the unique purity
of our deepest emotion.

That sanctity attained
when soulmate love is found, then bound,
how unprepared we were to learn
how abruptly life can turn
happiness around.

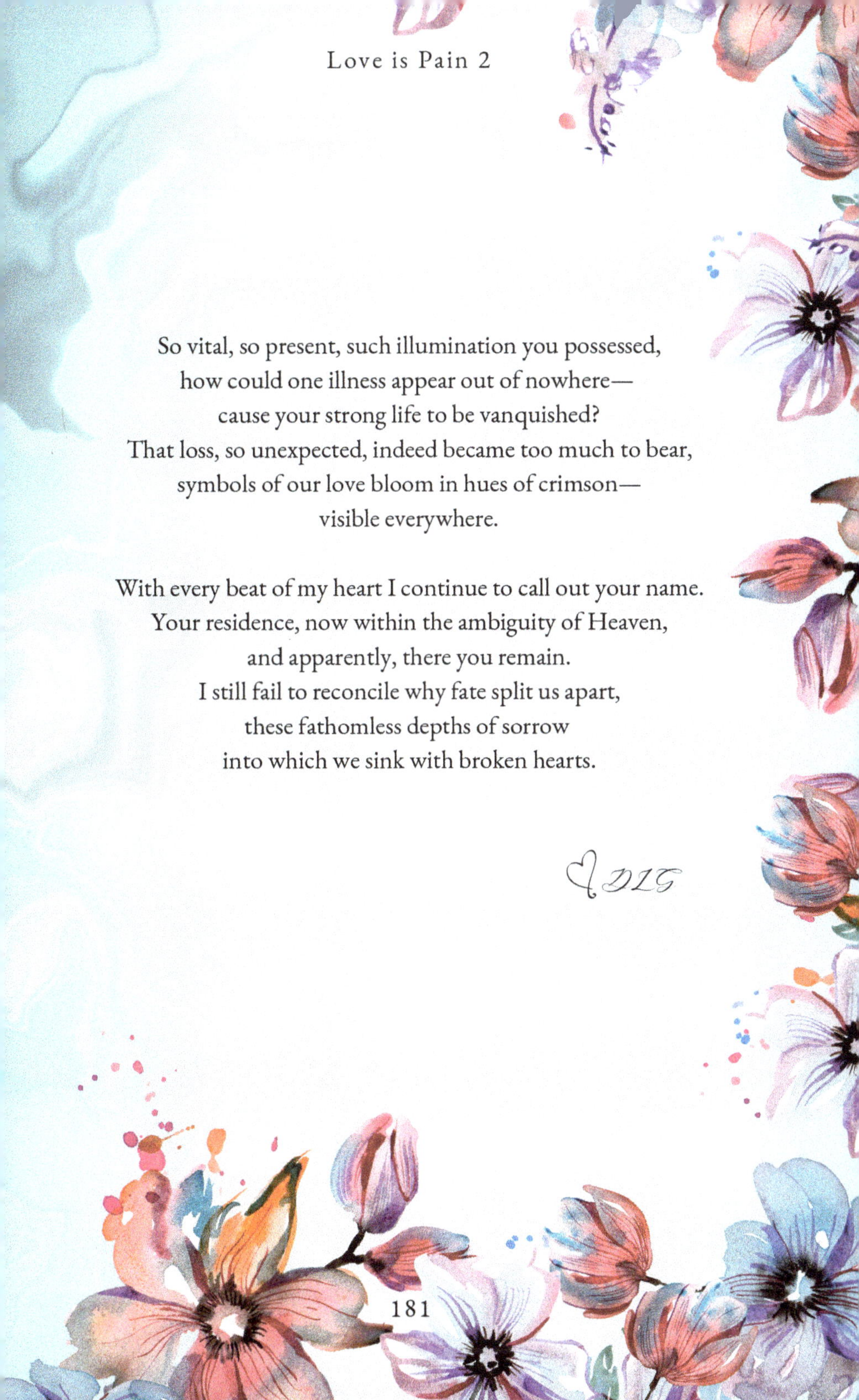

So vital, so present, such illumination you possessed,
how could one illness appear out of nowhere—
cause your strong life to be vanquished?
That loss, so unexpected, indeed became too much to bear,
symbols of our love bloom in hues of crimson—
visible everywhere.

With every beat of my heart I continue to call out your name.
Your residence, now within the ambiguity of Heaven,
and apparently, there you remain.
I still fail to reconcile why fate split us apart,
these fathomless depths of sorrow
into which we sink with broken hearts.

Diane Lipton Gollub

My profound mistake was in first
enabling you to possess my heart—my head—
to fill your vacantness.

Slithering in your unctuous way to consume me—your goal,
you narcissistically proceeded to attempt to seize all control
while diminishing my perceptions and perspectives—
in your attempts to make yourself whole;
a pathetic peon of a person emerged quickly, from your soul.

However, you erred in presuming me to be weak,
for what drew you to me was my formidable mystique.

I now declare you to be
a vacuous, vile, venomous replica of a human being
who leeches life from all
whom you deem as more intriguing.

Your alleged love;
like a black hole into which you have been submerged—
I pity those unfortunate women—
not savvy enough to perceive
that your wretched persona would unfold!

It was too late for too many;
as they were reduced to the dust that remained.
After encountering you—
all were driven insane.

<h1>I Cast Myself Free</h1>

With maniacal might, your attempts to restrict
my freedom to fly, my right to exist.
Through endless machinations,
trying to impose your will upon mine,
as though you believed you received permission
from somewhere Divine!

But, behold,
I cast myself free from the forbidding fetters you forged,
broke out, your oppression was assessed with my scorn.
I bid thee to find somewhere in your sorry soul,
the means to find happiness without demanding control.

DLG

'Twas the only home
I'd ever known,
grown up to see
family love depicted on TV,
that care that families share
in those films, displayed,
everywhere.
But this is a place
filled with disgrace,
a golden cacophony of love,
true sin lies within.

A Place Filled With Disgrace

Diane Lipton Gollub

Bloodshot Eyes

Hold it in
He cannot win
Harsh blows descend
Whilst I pretend
This torture ends
Struggling to appear unfazed
Within this abhorrence, staged
Violence is vented
My abuser demented
My blood is dripping
As tears start slipping
Summon forth my courage
Take hold of my mind
To travel through time
To a soothing place
Where I once found grace
Now trapped in this cage
Beneath secret rage
Should I emerge
Bloodshot eyes
Reflect this scourge

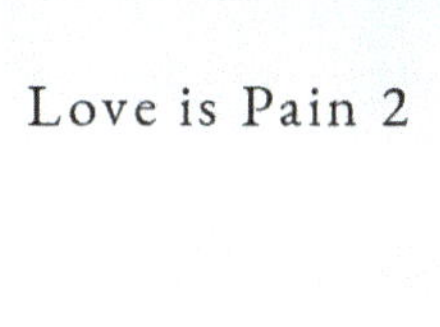

The Parameters of Our Psyche

Daily doses of destruction descending,
pointed pellets piercing procured protective veils,
struggling to survive the smoldering suffocation.
Trapped whilst immersed in our own perspectives,
it becomes hard sometimes
to see beyond the parameters of our own psyche.
Remaining haunted,
as nightmares begin to invade my days,
no beauty lies within the eyes of this beholder.
Upon struggling to seize some clarity of vision,
I become cognizant.
My home is now amongst wretched scoundrels and monstrous beings,
as I seem to have been born to heinous imperfection.
I have found my niche.

♡DLG

About
the
Author

Jimmy Broccoli

Jimmy Broccoli is a Library Branch Manager by day and a published poet by night with a mission to inspire his readers through imaginative poetic storytelling. His work has been featured in several publications and he has released three collections of poems - "Damaged", "Rabbits", & "Boy" and is the selector and editor of two poetry anthologies - "Spotlight" & "Encore. He enjoys walks on the beach and playing with puppies.

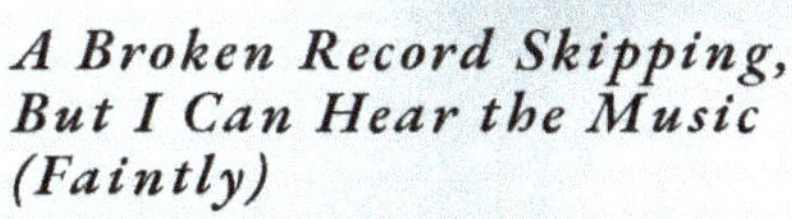

*A Broken Record Skipping,
But I Can Hear the Music
(Faintly)*

*Cyanide Gas - No Sarin
June 14, 2018*

Jimmy Broccoli

Jimmy Broccoli

A Broken Record Skipping,

But I Can Hear the Music (Faintly)

With my 100-day chip held tight in my trembling hand
I sit next to you on the deteriorating couch, lumpy and uncomfortable
I remain silent, looking down at the worn and stained carpet
with a universe of love, appreciation, and sorrow overwhelming my heart

My eyes have long cleared – I no longer begin my days with Visine
I've regained 8 of the 56 pounds I lost during the years I used
I'm submitting job applications, semi-respectable positions
that might make you proud

You deserve a guy, a man, who offers you picnics by the lake
Swans drifting elegantly upon the surface of the water
Perhaps an open bottle of wine, breathing in the fresh air
Future photographs, treasured, of you and him smiling, uncontrollably
You deserve the peanut butter sandwiches he will make for you
because they are your favorite
A tiny love note set beside your lunch,
with a heart and an arrow drawn through it
To remind you how much he loves you
A man who physically hurts when you are away from him

Saturday evenings, too frequently, ended with my head in the toilet
You, sitting beside me on the hard, cold bathroom floor
In an apartment without heat because I hadn't worked for weeks
or had forgotten to pay the bill

You telling me it's okay and me telling you I'd quit
But I wouldn't quit -
And I watched you as your future plans and aspirations
slowly, and painstakingly, swirled down with the toilet water
With my vomit circling down to the sewer,
taking with it your optimism
and your faith in my recovery and our future together

You've sacrificed everything – for me
You sit beside me now, your expression tired and worn
Then you smile at me anyway – it's strained, but genuine

I walk towards the front door, my packed bag zipped up and ready
You don't appear surprised, and you do not stand to protest
I suspect I've stolen your emotions over the years,
shooting them into my veins to die

You remain silent and still, your eyes following my every movement

Our old, unoiled, screen door creaks as it slowly shuts behind me
You do not follow me or call out my name

I think we both understand

Several feet down the street, walking towards my uncertain future
- I didn't hear it -
But (I imagine) you just audibly and painlessly exhaled –

Perhaps, for the first time in years

Cyanide Gas - No Sarin

Jimmy Broccoli

My mother's mind is a wilderness of confusion
She is lost, stumbling over jagged rocks, and finding no
clearing from among the crowded, skeletal trees
No breadcrumbs lie before her with whispered promises
to lead her back home
It's getting dark and the wolves are howling –
they are fast approaching, saliva dripping from their
hungry mouths

Within my hands is a basket, brilliant and blossoming –
filled with pretty flowers:
roses, dandelions, and lilacs
and offerings of unconditional and sempiternal love –

But - time is running out and the flowers in the basket
will soon begin to wither

Cyanide gas - no, sarin -

no, tetrodotoxin - no, sarin -

192

like was used on the Tokyo subway trains in 1995
I'm sitting, reluctantly and awkwardly,
in a corner of the Internet that can't be legal
Chat room conversations are scrubbed within seconds –
speak and read quickly -
Compound 1080 with an immediate muscle relaxer and coma-inducer
Pentobarbital -
the pink liquid in the syringe given to sickly animals at the vet
There must be no pain – no pain at all – no pain – no pain
- My computer screen glows before me in a darkened room –
the only sound is my fingertips on the keyboard,
searching for the unthinkable
The temperature is uncomfortable -
and I feel myself emotionally dying – slowly

I place a finger over my lips and shake my head
And speak, "shhhhh", softly and gently -
While looking at myself within the bathroom mirror

My reflection is shadowed -
and I cannot tell if I am angel or monster

continued

June 14, 2018

The chairs within Jason's Deli are hard and I cannot sit still
My mother and father sit across from me –
my sister beside me
(the conversation must remain happy, my dad tells us –
so my mother doesn't begin screaming again) –
we just calmed her down
Dementia is a demon –
it takes, and it takes, and it steals, and it devours,
and it claws, and it strips a person of their dignity and pride –
and it eats away memories
until there is little or nothing remaining on the plate
      "I love you so much, mom – and it's so good to see you," I speak
          It has been 5 years – and before that it had been 8

      The customer service cashier looks at us – at our table, occasionally
She looks worried and I understand. I occasionally look at her and smile
She doesn't believe my smile – but I'm confident we are communicating
The woman replacing the salad bowls at the end of the counter looks nervous
She gets it – I can tell – as she wells up and quickly walks to the back room

I look at my mother and pause
She sits in a wheelchair – a manual one – not an electric
Her dress is slightly twisted and disheveled –
and I don't know whether to fix it or not, so I remain in my seat
My mother knows who I am – but recognizes nobody else at the table
And I know this because she is suddenly frightened and frantic
She looks in my direction for comfort
"I'm here mom, I'm here."
I reach my hand across the table – and she, instinctively, takes it

Then -
She doesn't know which side of the fork to eat with –
so my dad assists her
And she does it reluctantly because she doesn't know who he is
And I know this is true because she says it out loud
to all of us and she says it loudly
She then turns to me,
"You're my son," my mother whispers
– I nod my head up and down
And can say no words in response
As I feel myself emotionally dying - slowly

continued

Jimmy Broccoli

"Mom, I'm here. I'm your son and I love you so very much."
"I love you too," she gets out, smiling genuinely
There are no more salad bowls at the end of the counter
and absolutely nobody in all directions fucking cares

Trash cans are receptacles for waste, garbage, and questionable ideas

At Jason's Deli, I throw away the blueprint –
the plan and the directions -
with the food I didn't eat
– on our way out the door -

"Mom", I speak aloud in my own head –
"I just can't – I love you and know you are miserable –
You are miserable all the time
Every day - every minute –
and for every confusing and agonizing second

and I just can't."

And because of this decision – she suffered for 2 ½ more years
Every day – every minute –
and for every confusing and agonizing second

Mother, mom –

"I am so sorry."
– tears falling from my hysterical eyes, forever

I just couldn't
I just couldn't

♡ JB

About the Author

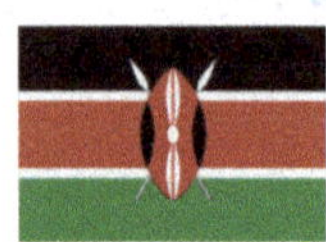

Blue Carrisole
@bluecarrisole

Blue Carrisole is a writer and poet raised in East Africa. Her writing is heavily influenced by the grief she experienced from losing her parents during her youth. Through her poetry, she seeks not only to process her own feelings but also to have her readers feel understood and connected to her work. Her poetry shows us what it means to have lived and explored the depths of love, pain, and death.

She has been published in several publications, including *Brave Voices Literary Magazine*, *Academy of the Heart and Mind*, *Rose Royal magazine, and Libero Magazine.* Her most notable award was the Best Writer of the Year, which she attained when she was 13, awarded to her by President Uhuru Kenyatta for a fictional short story she wrote based on the grieving process involved with the death of her mother.

Kisses Like Pain
As I Think of You
Don't Tell Anyone
Bounding Main
Suburban Sadness
My Anxiety and I
Silence to Speech
Chaos
Blue Carrisole

He kisses like pain with splinters of sorrow,
  saying he loves me today and he still will tomorrow.
  His fingers are warm
  I arch my back welcoming his lies.
  He holds me close, whispers so soft,
  and I forget that I cry.
  He gifts me with apologies, all labeled 'I'm very sorry,
  wrapped pretty with guilt,
  hoping to erase all the blood my cuts had spilled.
  But liar liar, my body's on fire
  as it recalls the memory of your fists,
  You hit me today, love me tomorrow,
  Then kiss me like pain and splinters of sorrow.

♡ BC

Kisses Like Pain

We were storms of fan-flames once.
You were red,
but I'm still blue—
burning out as embers,
hoping to create something new.

We were sublime souls, living on a pure, selfless streak,
a line of life that left us bleak.
Our smiles and laughter once echoed each other,
but, like everyone else,
you're now an everyday stranger.

We were broken puzzle pieces meant to make a whole,
until time said we couldn't fit.
All our affections now lie,
somewhat dead in a pit,
and I pray they rest in peace.

If feigned memories and their intensities
are all I have to hold,
then remember me...
as I think of you.

Blue Carrisole

Don't tell anyone,
but I'm having a hard time letting go.
It should be over.
It should have concluded.
The curtains should be closed by now.
The pain should have washed over me.
The longing should have left me.
I should be able to breathe,
hearing your name
without feeling like I'm disintegrating.

Don't tell anyone,
but the dark crypt I call my mind
has gone from being a canvas,
covered in demon faces painted blue,
to a wallpaper
illuminated by memories of you.

It should have ended
the moment I decided to let go.
But I'm still holding on.
Your name leaves prints
in the dusky corners of my mind,
in bright neon colors—
just to highlight
that I will never be free.

And I don't understand.
Maybe the memories are holding on to me,
maybe my unwillingness to relinquish
E V E R Y T H I N G
that relates to you
is just the recollections fighting against me.

I'm inhaling their old dust
that somehow feels new—
every single time.

And they're sipping on my mirth,
so they know, they'll survive.

Don't tell anyone,
but I'm sinking in the shallow pool
of tears I refuse, to cry
because I can't let you have that much power
over me.

It should have stopped
the moment I decided
that I could see you as less than nothing—
that I could erase you,
like you were never there,
like I never cared.

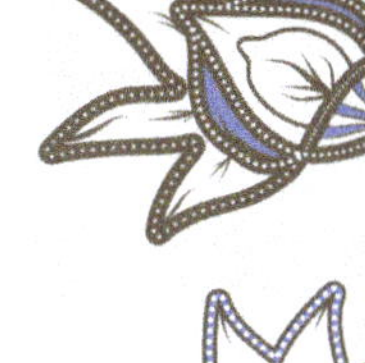

continued

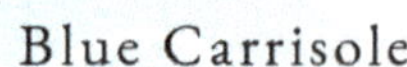

Blue Carrisole

Yet when I don't see you in my mind,
I feel you at the soles of my feet—
burning, rising through my veins
like the toxic blood that flows within me.

Just so you can reach my brain again,
wrap my thoughts in caution tape
labeled with your name.

And I can't release you from my bloodstream
when I exhale.

> So, don't tell anyone,
> but you're killing me.
> The toughest parts of me weep,
> the demons that unite me have turned
> their faces in disappointment.

Saying I don't deserve the devil horns
that stand below my halo,
because I'm an echo of the monster
I once was.

> I'm watching the wrecking ball swing,
> like it's a building it's destroying
> and not me.

I'm walking around, relaxed,
with my poker exterior,
like the destruction you caused is not
consuming me.

Please, don't tell anyone,
but you've disassembled me
and left me like
an unchronological masterpiece.

♡ BC

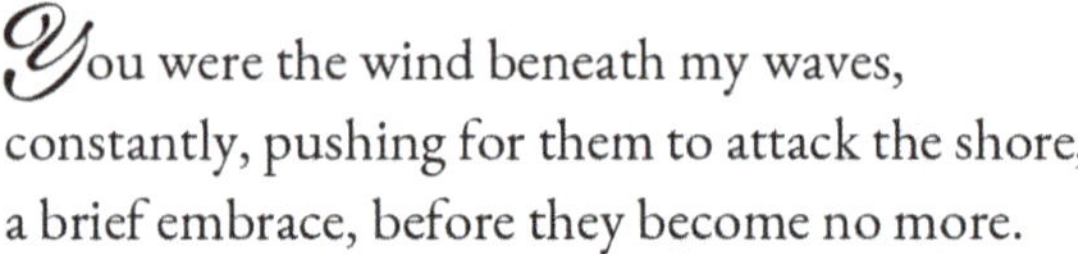

You were the wind beneath my waves,
constantly, pushing for them to attack the shore,
a brief embrace, before they become no more.

You were the silence in every storm,
between every lost sailor's scream and siren's song.

You were salt,
and I was the sea,
Every ounce of you is somehow embedded in me.

Now,
a seductive blue at the depth of dusk,
your shimmering view at the brink of dawn.
My waters lay still...
because you've lost where you belong.

Bounding Main

These suburban skies fall,
so we're covered in their blue.
Underneath the rain, roses are blemished red,
but then again, so are you...

These tulips stole the color from your halo,
but you're still heavenly.

These deserted suburban street lights faintly glimmer,
so we're covered in decaying yellow—ghosts of their shadows.
Underneath their dying glow, the concrete is mellow,
but then again, so am I...

These love-stricken lilies have stolen our memories,
but we're still a cursed treasury.

These long-winged suburban clouds bind us,
so we're covered in ultramarine and beryl.
Underneath the rain, I'm still the very same devil,
but then again, so are you...

This pencil clock sketched us together from the start,
but we're still two separate pieces of art.

Suburban Sadness

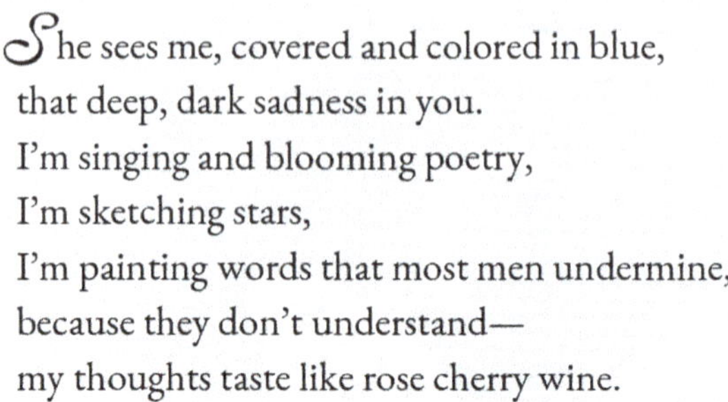

Blue Carrisole

My Anxiety and I

She sees me, covered and colored in blue,
that deep, dark sadness in you.
I'm singing and blooming poetry,
I'm sketching stars,
I'm painting words that most men undermine,
because they don't understand—
my thoughts taste like rose cherry wine.

My anxiety will see that, and she'll say, "You're mine,"
so I run to her when you reject me
because I realize she's the only one who'll accept me.
I'm stuck in a loop of codependency,
but I don't mind,
because that's just my anxiety, and I.

But when I try to be brave,
she slaps me with fear.
Suddenly, her love is unclear.
Inspiration deserts me,
so do the stories that could be.
The thoughts inside me scream, "I want to be free,"
but she won't let them go,
and so, neither do I.
I guess that's just my anxiety and I.

Dare I defy her,
she'll make me suffer.
Sometimes I sink in loneliness,
because I can't take her bossiness.
And she'll say, "Blue, remember I can see you
in a way nobody else does,
love in a way nobody else loves."

So I run to her because it's true,
I'm that kind of blue.
Everybody rejects me.
No one knows what to do with me.
I need her; it hurts, but she'll still accept me.
So I don't mind,
that's just my anxiety, and I.

When confidence visits me, we keep it a secret—
because she'll say I've been bad, been very bad.

I'll be blooming and singing poetry,
painting words and sketching stars that come alive,
With that *I wanna write* vibe—
stories for miles, days, and decades drive.
She says when you read them,
"You'll have that 'I don't understand' mind."

Quickly, confidence deserts me.
You don't know what to do with me.

Everybody rejects me,
but she'll still accept me.
We are stuck in a loop of codependency,
but we don't understand
because that's just my anxiety, and I.

"If you asked me to,
I'd fly to the sky with you,"
said Silence to Speech—
her love, she was trying to preach.
But Speech couldn't speak;
he feared their love was bleak.

"We'll climb ladders
to the clouds,"
silence spoke out loud,
but Speech couldn't speak;
with her, he'd remain meek.

"We'll go to where hopes grow
and rainbows beam,"
said Silence with a gleam.
But Speech couldn't speak;
he knew it was a fool's dream.

"Like the blue in the sky is limitless,
our adventures will be endless."
Silence went on, like they had the time,
but Speech couldn't speak;
her words were making him weak.

"It's too good for us, that's what you think,"
Silence realized, from the way he'd blink.
He nodded his head because Speech couldn't speak.
It was too good for them,
and he felt that a speaker like her didn't deserve a silence like him.

Blue Carrisole

Tell Chaos to rip me apart,
from the core of my not-so-delicate seams,
and put me back together again
when he sees fear running from the roots of my
clean arteries,
and circling around my dirty veins—
that she keeps encased in chains,
so my courage remains an obedient slave.

Tell him,
when he corrupts me, I'll dive deep into
E V E R Y T H I N G
he has to offer,
wear his toxicity like second skin,
then embrace the way it pricks me,
While he embraces me, and pricks me.

When these sheathed bones
keep my hopeful heart locked
within a demon's kiss
and an angel's touch,
and fear quivers
within the fluorescent corners of my mind.

Tell Chaos,
the cold warmth that comes with a foul state of mind,
when he's around,
is where I want to hide.

Patiently, I'll wait for him to speak,
then freely kneel before the mercy of his words,
when I feel his less-than-gentle breath
creeping across the surface of my skin.

And should these sheathed bones
still keep my hopeful heart locked within a demon's
kiss and an angel's touch,
then I'll abandon the idea of tranquility,
pull out the remaining knots of fear
still planted inside me,
and cage the left-over slivers of innocence within my soul,
then submit to chaos's peace,
because it's where I want to be.

Should chaos assimilate fear's power over me,
then I'll accept it
when he drapes me in prison stripes
of plain envy and monochromatic anarchy.

I'll undress the luminous parts of my mind,
who will bargain with my demons,
and the angels will be inclined
to release my heart,
so the hope desiccates,
and when it does,
in chaos's arms
will I hide.

213

About the Author

Anila Bukhari

Anila Bukhari The Unstoppable Force for Change "
Anila Bukhari, a young girl with an unwavering spirit and an unmatched drive to make a difference, has left an indelible mark on the world. Her journey as an advocate for children's rights, a champion of girls' education, a devoted teacher, a compassionate humanitarian, a philanthropist, and a peace ambassador is nothing short of extraordinary.

At just 20 years old, Anila embarked on a writing journey that captivated readers across 50 countries. Her powerful words have earned her numerous accolades, recognizing her exceptional contributions to humanity. Anila's books shed light on global issues, offering solutions, and placing a particular focus on the importance of girls' education.

Anila's impact extends far beyond the pages of her books. She has personally educated 1,000 refugees and orphans in Uganda, establishing small wooden libraries in remote areas to provide underprivileged girls with access to education. Her compassion for others has also led her to donate hair wigs to cancer patients, bringing comfort and smiles during their challenging journeys.

Anila's groundbreaking work in advocating for girls' education has led her to introduce the world to the Girls' Education Awareness Day, celebrated in 11 different countries. Her unwavering determination to educate every girl is a testament to her vision for a brighter future.

Through her writing, Anila instills hope and encouragement, empowering individuals to overcome obstacles and reach for their dreams. Her impact on the world is immeasurable, and her legacy will continue to inspire generations to come. Anila's unstoppable force for change is a true testament to the power of youth, compassion, and determination.

Anila Bukhari

Anila Bukhari

Wish of
A Girl

In a humble home of dust and clay
lives a young girl with a heart full of play.
She spends her days in the company of animals
and finds solace in their gentle rhythms.

Her eyes sparkle with a desire to see
beyond the limits of her humble stage.
Social norms bound her wings,
preventing her from spreading them and flying.

She cries into her grandmother's pillow
as she wishes for a world that is more than just hollow.
She longs to be a shining star,
but the weight of tradition holds her back.

She writes her wishes in the dirt
and hopes for a future that is not dirt.
Peace evades her grasp
as she struggles to break free from the past.

Oh Moon, Please Grace Me

Oh, dear Moon, please grace me with your presence,
I long to embrace you, my guiding luminescence.
In the darkest of times, you're my shining light,
You witness my tears when the world sleeps tight.

Can you, oh Moon, ease my sorrow's grip?
Can you bring happiness to my empty basket's tip?
In this struggle called life, I find no respite,
Why am I unsatisfied, burdened with inner plight?

Someone within me cries out, loud and clear,
Yearning to silence the anger, the fear.
Why was I born into this world so tough?
Faced with difficulties, feeling so rough.

But amidst the challenges that surround,
There's hope to be found, love to astound.
Together, we'll navigate this winding road,
Finding strength within, as our stories unfold.

So, dear friend, hold on and don't despair,
For life's mysteries, we'll bravely dare.
In the face of adversity, we shall rise,
Embracing the journey, with determination in our eyes.

Anila Bukhari

Education's Light

In solitude she weeps, a girl so sad,
For her father's love, she yearns to have.
He despises her education, so it seems,
Denying her dreams, shattering her self-esteem.

She cooks his meals, irons his clothes,
Yet he denies her the path she chose.
Tears fall like raindrops, staining her face,
As she writes her diary in the still of space.

In the dead of night, she studies with care,
Hiding from her father's disapproving glare.
But suddenly he stirs, awakening from sleep,
And finds his daughter, studying deep.

Anger fills his voice, his actions so violent,
"Why do you study? You were born for servile ascent!
Your place is in the kitchen, not an office or school!
You don't deserve freedom, you're a servant, a fool!"

His hand strikes her face, leaving behind a mark,
But she refuses to surrender, to stay in the dark.
She cries in her bed, her spirit bruised,
Yet her determination cannot be diffused.

With each blow, her resolve grows stronger,
She continues her studies, striving for longer.
And as she achieves the highest of marks,
Her father's heart fills with regret, his conscience sparks.

He realizes the wrongs he has done,
How he mistreated his daughter, his precious one.
In her success, he finally sees,
The beauty of her dreams, the strength she frees.

Apologies spill from his lips, expressing remorse,
He finally understands the power of her course.
She forgives but never forgets the pain,
As she embraces her education's gain.

For in her triumph, she finds her voice,
A testament to her strength, her choice.
No longer confined by her father's disdain,
She rises above, her freedom she'll maintain.

♡AB

Anila Bukhari

In the depths of winter's icy embrace,
A poor boy selling eggs, with humble grace.
No shoes adorned his weary, calloused feet,
Yet hopes and dreams within his heart did meet.

Through rural lands he ventured, day by day,
Facing struggles, pain and grief that came his way.
As other children went to school with ease,
He persevered, his hope he did not cease.

On late foggy nights, in darkness he'd roam,
Boiling eggs, offering warmth and comfort as his own.
With no electricity to light his way,
He pedaled his bicycle, night turning to day.

Adversity struck, animals of the land did fight,
Beating him down, oh, what a cruel sight.
But still, he rose, undeterred by this plight,
For his determination burned with a fierce light.

Broken Boy

With meager earnings, he saved every cent,
His dream of education, his heart firmly bent.
One fateful day, fortune smiled upon his plight,
Admission granted, his future shining bright.

By day, he studied, devouring knowledge's feast,
By night, he sold his eggs, his soul released.
Through hardships endured, his spirit did rise,
Defying the odds, with unyielding eyes.

In the depths of winter's cold, he found his way,
A poor boy's journey, his path to display.
With each boiled egg, a step closer to his dream,
A testament of hope, against the harshest of extremes.

In the field of sunflowers, amidst the storm,
a nest, a haven, I chanced upon, worn.
A pigeon, radiant, in the waves it danced,
beautiful, yet pained, by man's cruel stance.

Oh, the hurt inflicted by humanity's woe,
why do they harm, why do they sow?
Insulting animals, tarnishing our kind.
Oh, how I yearn for a world more kind.

A walk so serene, a vision anew,
Where tears are banished, poverty too.
No violence lurking, no shadows of despair,
Just raindrops caressing, a tender affair.

Cozy winters, not too cold to bear,
where teeth don't chatter, but warmth we share.
Yet, child labor persists, an unjust plight.
Oh, pigeon, your wings bring solace in sight.

For when I stumble upon a nest in the storm,
With trees swirling, leaves taking their form,
I cradle the sparrow, so frail and weak,
dreaming of a night, foggy and mystique.

In this nocturnal haze, an old woman may appear,
Bestowing upon me a stick, magic sincere.
A wand to transform my pain, to heal my heart,
to mend the wounds, and grant a fresh start.

222

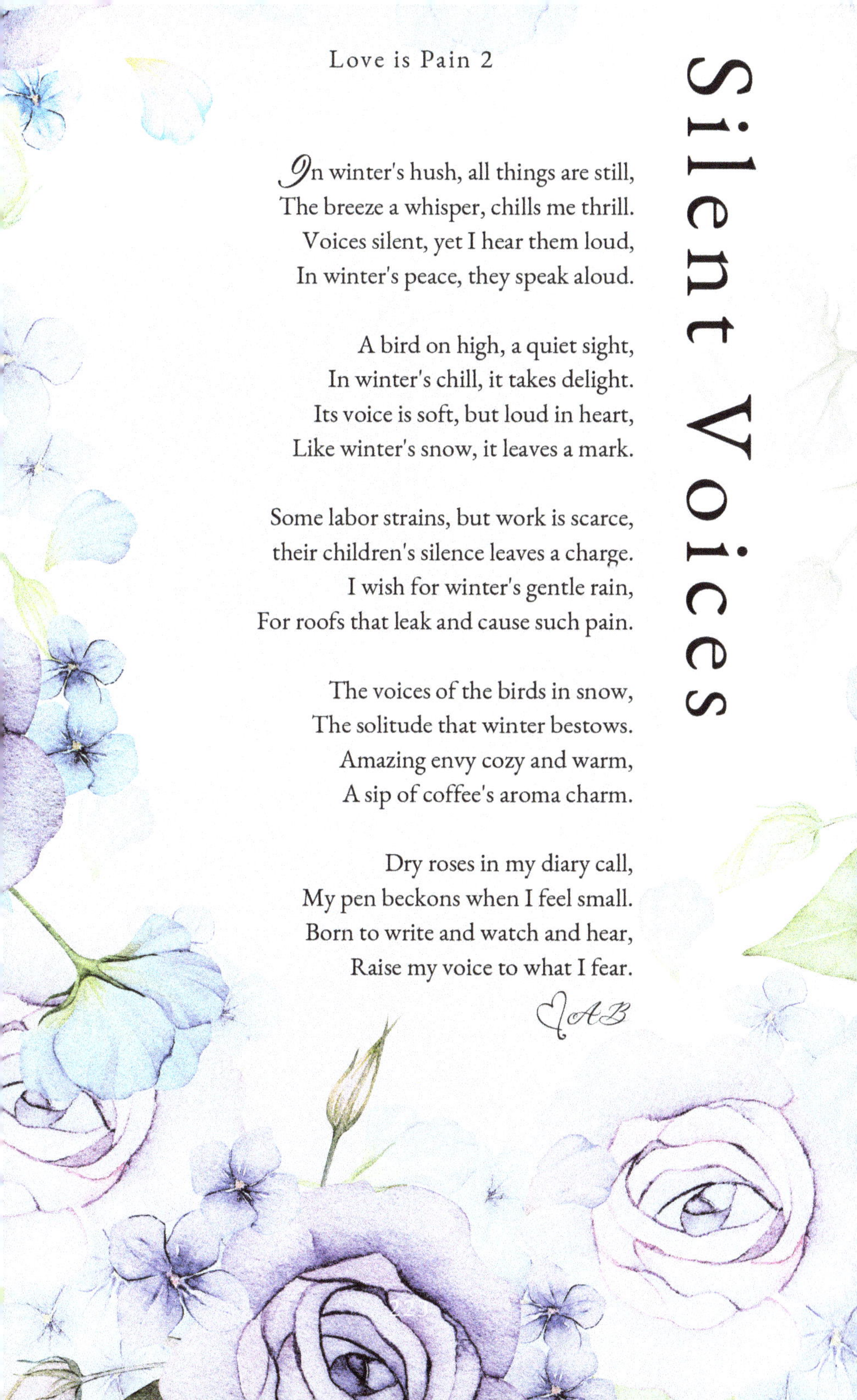

In winter's hush, all things are still,
The breeze a whisper, chills me thrill.
Voices silent, yet I hear them loud,
In winter's peace, they speak aloud.

A bird on high, a quiet sight,
In winter's chill, it takes delight.
Its voice is soft, but loud in heart,
Like winter's snow, it leaves a mark.

Some labor strains, but work is scarce,
their children's silence leaves a charge.
I wish for winter's gentle rain,
For roofs that leak and cause such pain.

The voices of the birds in snow,
The solitude that winter bestows.
Amazing envy cozy and warm,
A sip of coffee's aroma charm.

Dry roses in my diary call,
My pen beckons when I feel small.
Born to write and watch and hear,
Raise my voice to what I fear.

♡ AB

Anila Bukhari

Confronting Child Poverty

In the shadows of despair, where innocence is lost,
child poverty's grip, a battle to exhaust.
But in the darkest nights, a flicker of hope remains,
a world united, breaking poverty's chains.

Let's join hands, ignite compassion's flame,
empower every child, for they're not to blame.
With love as our guide, we'll bridge the divide,
together we'll conquer, with strength amplified.

AB

Girls' Education Soars

Like butterflies, they flutter, seeking the sky,
Girls' education takes flight, reaching new highs.
Their minds, a river, flowing with knowledge and grace,
Lit by the firefly of learning, illuminating their space.

In the moon's gentle glow, their dreams take flight,
Girls empowered, breaking barriers with all their might.
Let's nurture their minds, like flowers in bloom,
Educating girls, a world transformed, a brighter future to consume.

AB

Anila Bukhari

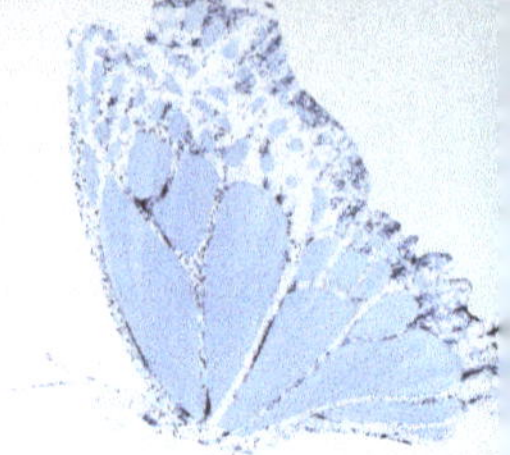

Guardians of Love

In the tapestry of life, their love gently weaves,
Parents, the guiding stars, our hearts they relieve.
Their care and wisdom, like a comforting embrace,
Let's cherish their presence, never leave them in solace.

For in their arms, we find solace and protection,
Their love, a beacon, guiding us in every direction.
Through the trials and joys, they stand by our side,
With unwavering support, their love cannot hide.

In their selfless devotion, an eternal flame,
Parents' love, a treasure, beyond any worldly claim.
Let's honor their sacrifices, in every single way,
For their love enriches our lives, day after day.

So let us embrace them, with gratitude and care,
For the importance of parents, beyond compare.
In their presence, let us always strive to be,
A reflection of the love they have given us so freely.

As we walk through life's journey, hand in hand,
May we never leave them alone, in any land.
For their love is a gift, a precious golden thread,
Guiding us, protecting us, until our days are shed.

A Tribute to Women's Empowerment

With strength and grace, she takes her stand,
A force to be reckoned with, a power so grand.
Unyielding and fierce, she breaks every chain,
Women's empowerment, a triumph that shall remain.

In her dreams, she finds the courage to soar,
Defying expectations, she opens every door.
Her voice echoes, a symphony of might,
As she fights for equality, in every fight.

Let's celebrate her spirit, her resilience untold,
Women's empowerment, a story to be bold.
Together we rise, hand in hand we unite,
For a world where her dreams shine infinitely bright.

♡ AB

Anila Bukhari

I Found Nothing

My love is so far from me, distant in his ways,
He didn't care, he didn't call, my soul in disarray.
He didn't think about my emotions, my heart left astray,
He didn't give me hope, love, or care, a price I had to pay.

I respected and cared for him, with all that I possess,
But in return, I found nothing, just emptiness, I confess.
So I learned, don't give your heart to anyone,
Don't love those who don't deserve your precious care, my dear one.

Goodbye to those who don't care, who don't hold my heart's flame,
I'm left feeling sad and lost, aching in my own pain.
But amidst the darkness, I've realized one thing,
To care for your own heart, a lesson love does bring.

So, I bid adieu to the ones who didn't see,
The worth of my love, the depth of my plea.
In the stillness and sorrow, I find strength anew,
To guard my heart with caution, to myself, I'll stay true.

For in this journey of love, there lies a sacred art,
To cherish our own souls, to heal and mend each part.
So, farewell to the apathy, the indifference that stings,
I'll walk with resilience, the melody true love sings.

My love may be distant, but my heart still beats strong,
I'll nurture its essence, for it has been wronged.
So, free from the chains of unrequited desire,
I'll find solace in self-love, my spirit shall aspire.

For in the end, it is I who holds the key,
To my own happiness, my own love's decree.
And though my love may be far, I'll find peace within,
For my heart deserves care, a love that's genuine.

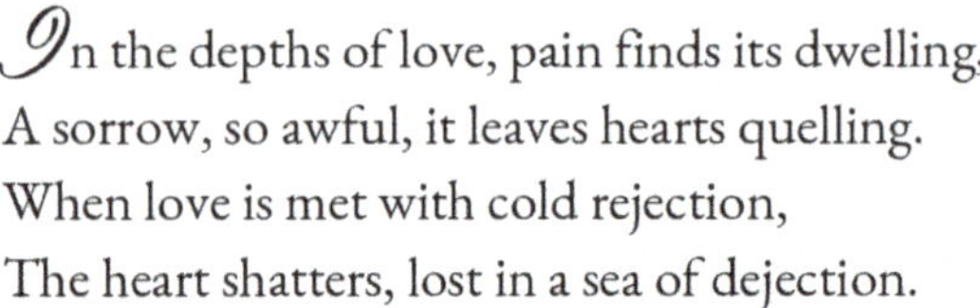

Anila Bukhari

Love's Wound

In the depths of love, pain finds its dwelling,
A sorrow, so awful, it leaves hearts quelling.
When love is met with cold rejection,
The heart shatters, lost in a sea of dejection.

I longed for him, but he did not call,
His indifference, like a bitter downfall.
In illness, I withered, unable to thrive,
For without his love, I felt barely alive.

But love, it seems, cared not for my plight,
Leaving me stranded in the darkest of nights.
I yearned for solace, a glimmer of hope,
Yet love's cruel grip refused to let me cope.

I learned, too late, the cost of my affection,
That love can break, leaving naught but dejection.
I lost everything, my heart torn asunder,
And now, I know not if I can recover.

For love, it seems, is a painful endeavor,
Bringing anguish that rends us forever.
In shattered pieces, we try to find peace,
But love's cruel game grants no sweet release.

So I, in this moment, make a solemn vow,
To guard my heart, to never allow
Love's treachery to consume me again,
For I have learned that love is a pain.

Yet still, deep within,
a flicker remains,
A longing for love,
despite its cruel strains.
But I tread with caution,
my heart wrapped in steel,
Knowing that love's wounds
are not easily healed.

♡ AB

About
the
Author

Michelle Chermaine Ramos

Michelle Chermaine Ramos is a versatile Canadian artist, author, and journalist of Filipino-Spanish-Japanese descent. Her creative journey spans a wide spectrum, encompassing fine arts, jewelry design, and literary pursuits. Drawing inspiration from her multicultural roots, Michelle Chermaine's work is a tapestry of influences that reflect her vibrant personal narrative. Her formative years spent in the Middle East, along with her deep fascination for various cultures and faiths, have shaped her artistic vision. Through her art, she aims to bridge cultural divides and encourage a deeper appreciation of our shared human experience. Her dedication to promoting understanding doesn't stop with her art. Her career has encompassed roles as a TV/radio host and print reporter with a special focus on covering news in the areas of art, culture, entertainment, martial arts, social justice, business, and other matters of interest to immigrant communities in Canada. An inspirational storyteller, she has interviewed and spotlighted the success stories of local and global trailblazers, creatives, and entrepreneurs.

Connect with her online:
- Instagram: @michellechermaine
- Facebook: http://www.facebook.com/MichelleChermaineArt/
- Website: http://www.michellechermaine.com
- E-mail: info@michellechermaine.com

Michelle Chermaine Ramos

Michelle Chermaine Ramos

Woken, Not Broken

You thought you had broken me
the last time we spoke.

You walked out the door
expecting me to implore you
to please,
please
come back.

As if my lack of a reaction
over the way you acted
—after you unfriended and blocked me
—meant that you had won that argument.

You thought the silent treatment
was a power move.

Ooh...
how fun was it
when it proved to be wrong
as soon as you turned right around
and threw a fit,
furiously knocking,
demanding to be let back in.

As if *you*
had the right
to decide when you can
just waltz in and out of my life.

As if unblocking me
and insisting on opening that door
should automatically
restore things to the way they were before.

Oh...but that door is locked now!

Never have I ever
brought the trash back in
—especially
after it has so conveniently taken itself out.

Let that fact sink into your head.

I'm not broken—*but I have woken,*
and am way, way wiser instead.

And I have you to thank for it.

Michelle
Chermaine
Ramos

Michelle Chermaine Ramos

Heartstrings

She has heartstrings
made of piano wire
that sing sweet beauty
bright as fire,

but when men treat her
as they oughtn't,
double as some fine garrotes
leaving wretched hearts to rot.

Torn out.

Trodden.

And forgotten.

Michelle Chermaine Ramos

Don't Forget Yourself

A comforting touch, a listening ear,
a cheerful word to clear sad tears,
kind eyes that see and understand,
the priceless gift of a helping hand.
Ever so present to hold near and dear,
together through weather both stormy and clear.

In being their haven, you must recall
you cannot always do it all.
Don't let your energy and time dry up.
You cannot pour from an empty cup.
To your own needs too, you must attend,
the way you would a cherished friend.
This crucial lesson you must learn:
You deserve the same love you give in return.

Michelle Chermaine Ramos

236

Idols Less Divine

For those beguiled
by misguided eyes
and desperately pine
for faces fair and luscious hair,
and bewitching lips like wine,
and chiseled bodies in their prime
that acquit fine twits of foolish crimes
by blinding minds to overlook
the beasts behind sly beauty's hooks...

Know hope still springs for those ensnared
once faded raiments strip souls bare,
unveiling idols less divine,
for none is as sobering as time.

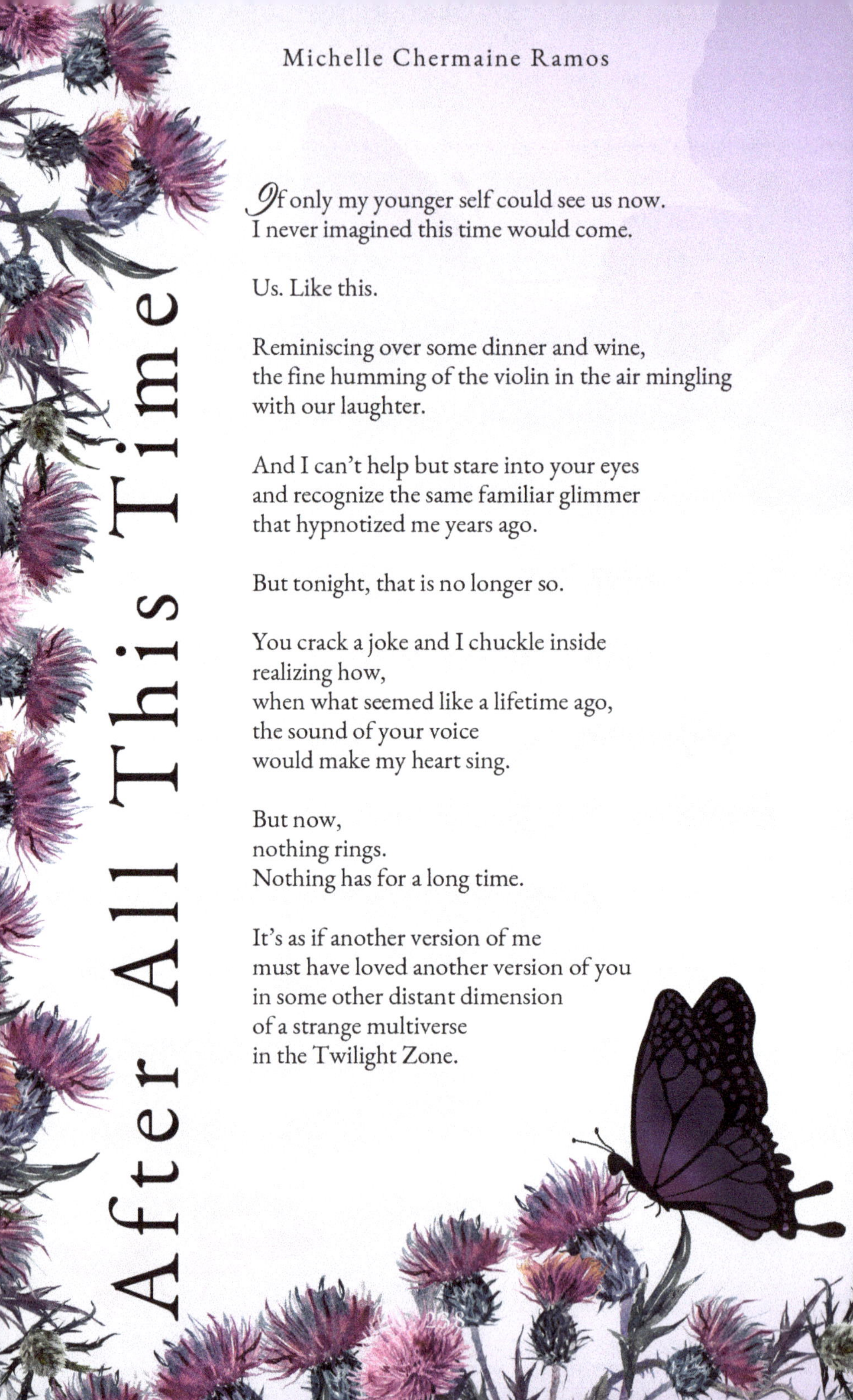

Michelle Chermaine Ramos

If only my younger self could see us now.
I never imagined this time would come.

Us. Like this.

Reminiscing over some dinner and wine,
the fine humming of the violin in the air mingling
with our laughter.

And I can't help but stare into your eyes
and recognize the same familiar glimmer
that hypnotized me years ago.

But tonight, that is no longer so.

You crack a joke and I chuckle inside
realizing how,
when what seemed like a lifetime ago,
the sound of your voice
would make my heart sing.

But now,
nothing rings.
Nothing has for a long time.

It's as if another version of me
must have loved another version of you
in some other distant dimension
of a strange multiverse
in the Twilight Zone.

After All This Time

Love is Pain 2

How comforting this is to know
that *we* are now ghosts.

It's amazing how some things
always stay the same,
as it's magically liberating
how some don't.

Your love is here.

That place is no longer my place.
Your heart is no longer mine,
as mine is no longer yours.
That door has been closed
for some time now.

Time has faithfully sewn old wounds
and cured us sooner
than I ever believed it could.
Oh, how much we have grown!

My heart overflows seeing
that things are as they're meant to be.
The distance between us now
the same as your love sitting in front of me.
And I'm happy you've chosen wisely.

continued

As I share a slice of cake with your soulmate,
we chat excitedly all night
about love,
life,
and everything in between.
I marvel at how we relate over how much
we appreciate the same things.

Then it struck me.

How,
for those hours,
I forgot that *you* were even right there.

How do you measure this miracle?

Once upon a time,
when you and I ended,
it felt like I would never mend.

And now,
each time I see you both very much in love,
my heart swells above all measure
treasuring how lucky I am
to be doubly blessed with such good friends.

To The Man Who Was Told He Feels 'Too Much'

Just take a moment to consider
all the battles you've weathered that
crushed lesser men. How, then, can you not
know how your kind and loving heart,
surviving all of this and shining for
others against all odds, was
never your weakness, but a
gift of strength bestowed upon only the
ablest, noblest souls?

The God who made you installed His
enduring love in you to light the night into the dawn.
Shine on! Shine on! *Shine on!*

Michelle
Chermaine
Ramos

About the Author

Julie Ann Keleher

@mykindamidnight

I am a poet who loves Midnight and Coffee, and all the strange things in life. I am also a mother of two amazing children. I love spending time with family and friends. I started writing when I was seven years old about magical worlds where nobody would suffer. I am an advocate for many different health issues and for the elderly. I tell all my secrets to the moon, and the stars hold onto my prayers. "Poetry is not just a word, poetry is meant to be heard! " When I see something I just love I say, "Oh now that's "mykindamidnight" !

Instagram handle @mykindamidnight

I Needed To Save Me
You Could Gravel A Road
Zombie Heart Song
Wasted Love
Tommy
Take Me Home
I Shouldn't Have
to Change for You
Blankie
Julie Ann Keleher

Julie Ann Keleher

When you said that you loved me,
you painted my heart red—
but every lie that you told
slowly started killing me off
until breathing seemed impossible.

With a heart that felt dead.

I could fake pretty eyes with makeup,
but then tears would stain my clothes.
I just needed the answer.
I thought, **Why would you do this to me?**
At one point, I was your undying rose.
But I needed to save **me**, and to do that,
 I had to stop saving **you**.

That's what a rose does.
The thorns are for safety—
or they would be all dying too.

244

You could gravel a road
with all the lies that you've told,
the only person who could handle that drive—
is you—
with all the rotten twists, turns,
and curves that you spew.

Why would anyone ever travel
that road with you?

You make everything sound like—
it's got the most impeccable view.

That smile of yours
could charm the most venomous snake,
but just like venom,
your love was vile.
Another wrong turn
that led to heartbreak and denial...

♡JAK

Julie Ann Keleher

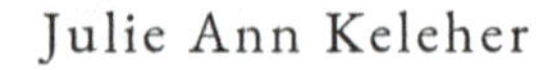

Quick to judge,
I did not budge.
Your words were fierce,
you fired them well.
Dancing like demons,
inside your heart from hell.

What you did not know,
was that I've been here before.
I waged a war,
with the devil before,
and I won—with scars that
were deeper than most people's views.
You slashed and cursed and cut a few, new.

I just closed my eyes,
and banished you, too.
Pain like that doesn't belong—
it eats out our hearts like a zombie heart song.

♡ JAK

Zombie Heart Song

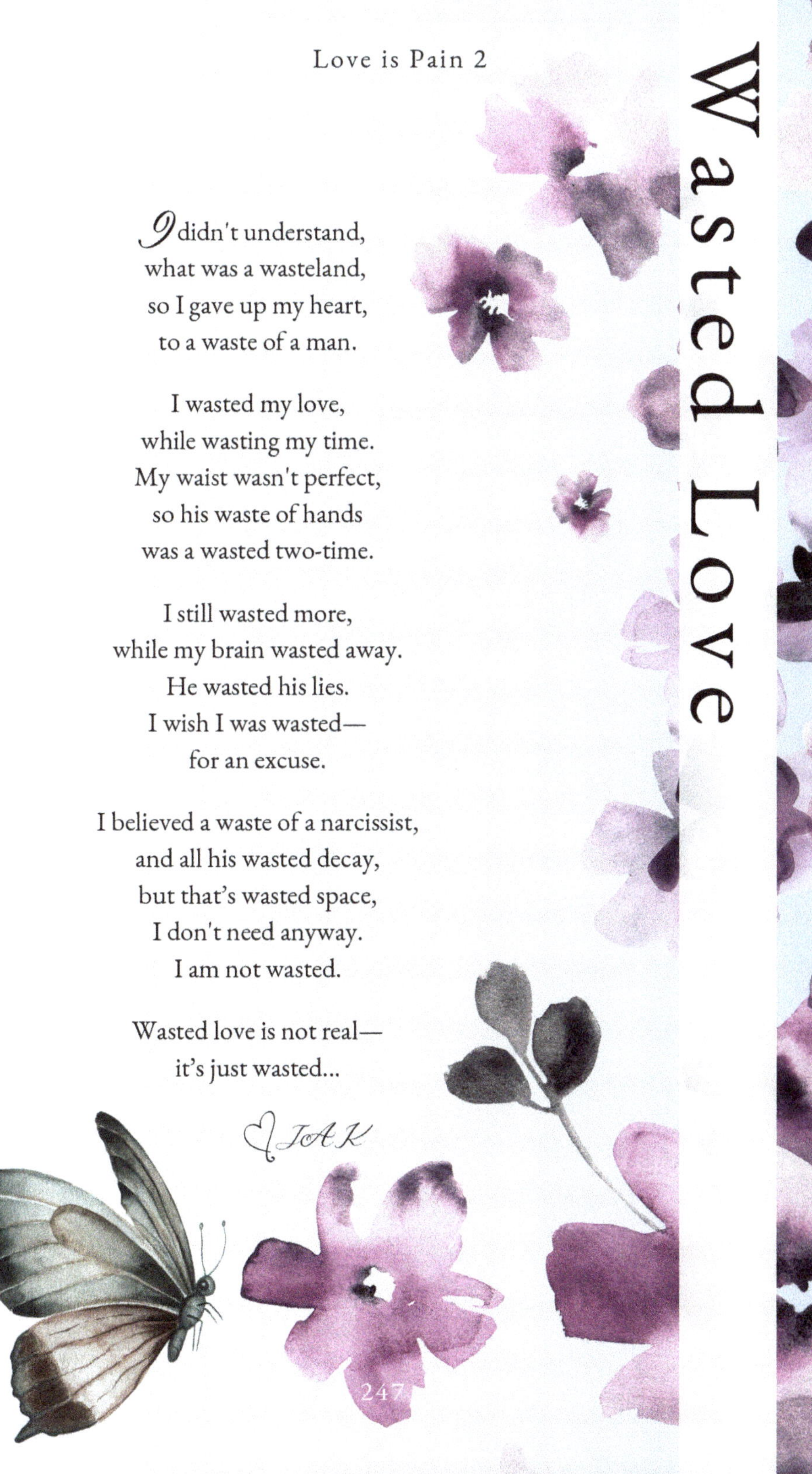

Wasted Love

I didn't understand,
what was a wasteland,
so I gave up my heart,
to a waste of a man.

I wasted my love,
while wasting my time.
My waist wasn't perfect,
so his waste of hands
was a wasted two-time.

I still wasted more,
while my brain wasted away.
He wasted his lies.
I wish I was wasted—
for an excuse.

I believed a waste of a narcissist,
and all his wasted decay,
but that's wasted space,
I don't need anyway.
I am not wasted.

Wasted love is not real—
it's just wasted...

JAK

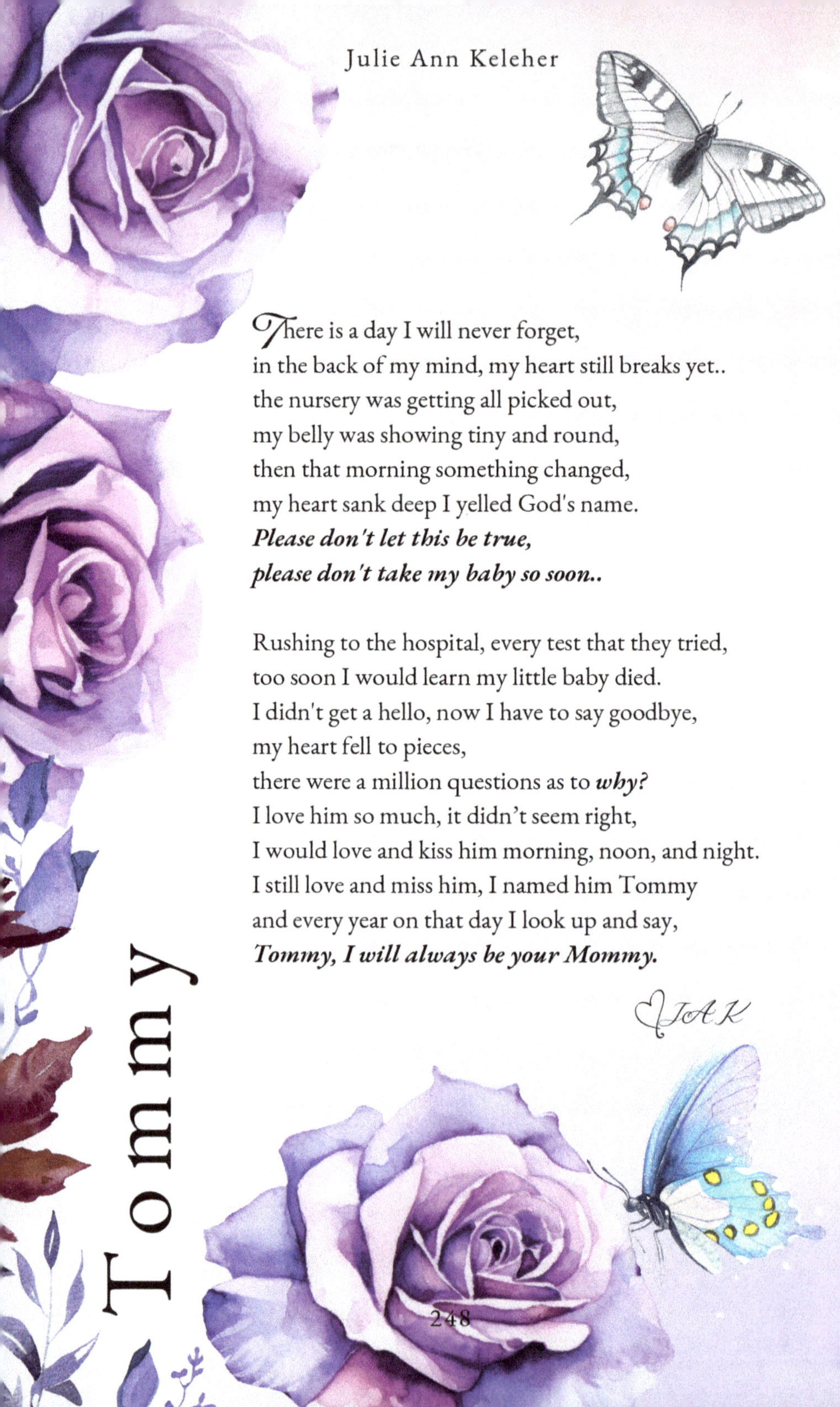

Julie Ann Keleher

There is a day I will never forget,
in the back of my mind, my heart still breaks yet..
the nursery was getting all picked out,
my belly was showing tiny and round,
then that morning something changed,
my heart sank deep I yelled God's name.
Please don't let this be true,
please don't take my baby so soon..

Rushing to the hospital, every test that they tried,
too soon I would learn my little baby died.
I didn't get a hello, now I have to say goodbye,
my heart fell to pieces,
there were a million questions as to **why?**
I love him so much, it didn't seem right,
I would love and kiss him morning, noon, and night.
I still love and miss him, I named him Tommy
and every year on that day I look up and say,
Tommy, I will always be your Mommy.

JAK

Time is of the essence...

Three O'clock on the dot,
not a second late.
We meet almost every night
through some twist of fate.

I wonder if I am dreaming,
and you try to play on my fears,
or if my life is like I think,
where I am both monster and Angel.

And that's why I am here:
I can fight your demons.
I stand firm, up against mine.

We will never know what it is about this life
that has so many on the run.
The sun is warm, yet I adore the moon.

Three O'clock, you make me feel not alone.
One day, when you find me,
it will be to just take me
home...

Take Me Home

Julie Ann Keleher

Do you like to drink coffee?
'Cause I sure do.
Do you like to look at the moon?
'Cause I sure do.
Do you like to love everybody?
'Cause I sure do.
And, if you love me,
then I shouldn't have to change for you.

I will always be a bit giddy,
and talk too much,
and walk too slow,
and take my time...
But if you're mine, then I love you,
and I shouldn't have to change for you.

Love is funny that way sometimes,
you meet and fall in love,
and all is great—
everything is fine.
But then, you want me to change into you,
and I shouldn't have to.

Because a heart is a heart,
and a mind is a mind,
and if you love me, like you said you do,
then I shouldn't have to change a thing
to love you.
Because I love you,
and I shouldn't have to change for you.

JAK

Blankie

I wanted to be your blankie,
to keep you safe and warm.
I took all the torture,
you received no harm.
But, just like blankies do,
pieces of me fell to the ground.
I was left to find myself,
your life kept moving on.

JAK

Julie Ann Keleher

There are layers of my soul
that could make you turn black.

Blacker than a night without a touch of Moon.

Blacker than those eyes whose stars have been lost
to the cost of a lover's war.

Blacker than the depths of the shadows of depression
when you feel the failure that you did all you could,
but love doesn't live there anymore.

Blacker than the dreams where sleep used to live,
and now you toss and turn.

Black in that heart where all you want
is for a love so great to pick you up
and life, for once, returns...

JAK

Black As Night

You hit where the soul meets the heart,
and either you fall in, or you fall apart,
naturally curving at every savory bend.

If this—a dream requiem—read me until the end,
not on speed dial, just linger with my worded ghosts
as you have been so deeply plunged into,
lovingly seeded, only to fall away as I back into you,
my intertwined, delirious mind.

Read those lines, strum accordingly,
and hear the bass drip from the melancholy
of your passionate lips.

Oh, you were so beautiful—
slow, but quick to enrich
every waking minute, and every minute second,
to display your lovered lover's affection,
the one tip-toeing through barbed wire and ashes,
hide and seek the specialty after dark,
blowing kisses, lighting spark after spark,
whiskey tipsy, never soaring or arching higher
than your tedious palpitations of blood vibration,
getting burned by Hades' fire.

Fall In Or Fall Apart

Julie Ann Keleher

Writing my pangs setting them free,
from this black heart that has encrypted me.
I cut away pieces, every night to give the dark sky,
I say, "Go away heartache, you are free now so am I."

Little by little I see the sky twinkle;
I think saying it's time to let go of the bars too,
but I am not sure, who they are keeping safe yet—
me or you...

JAK

$\mathcal{I}$ slept, as if you bid me well.
Out of this limited time,
in our lamented hell.
You said you never would leave,
but now you have sinned against yourself.

Amongst the fairytales,
you are just the fucking shelf.
You just sit there, gathering dust,
always lying in the shadows
But last night in my sleep—
I walked right out of the fucking gallows...

♡ JAK

I Walked Right Out

Julie Ann Keleher

Shall it be true
that this is the Blue Moon,
where lovers debut
like serendipity?
Right place, right time,
right smile, so divine.
The chance to feel it all,
or hide in the shadows—
in the cracks of the walls...
It is the desire of true fire
that lies in the heart.
You must proceed
in order for love to start.
A chance encounter from a stranger's face,
feeling like you've known them
from another time, another place.
A Blue Moon captures the event;
this is what makes it so special.
You feel this in your soul,
as if you have opened a time capsule.
A gift for love.
A chance encounter.
Serendipity.
Once in a Blue Moon.
A life full of love thereafter...

256

The Pain In My Being

Trigeminal neuralgia-
You didn't care if I was black or white,
you caught me off guard, it was a hell of a fright.

I thought I was dying, I thought I was cursed.
Too soon I would learn—it's a battle I couldn't reverse.

OH MY GOSH! WHAT THE HELL!
NO WAY! THIS CAN'T BE TRUE!
How can someone live through
so much pain with a demon like you?!

Then I realized I would have to tell you I am boss.
Yes, you will still hunt me, but I will never be caught.
You can zap, stab, burn, and make me insane.
My little secret you don't know, each battle is my gain.
I have you TN, yes that is your name.

Whenever you hit me, make me rock, scream, and cry,
here's what you don't know— that you lose every battle
and your pain is my high.

See I have you, you will NEVER have me!
One day I will be rid of you, just wait and see.

JAK

About the Author/ Curator/ Editor

Brandy Lane
@wherebeautifullives

Brandy Lane has lived most of her life in Indiana and Colorado, where she resides with her husband and four children. She published her first book, *Where Beautiful Loves*, in December 2020 under her imprint Where Beautiful Inks. Just after the release of her first book, she discovered anthologies as an option for publishing and has since had poetry pieces included in over three dozen publications. Publications include *Poetry 365 by RDW* (both abridged and unabridged editions) for November, December, January, February, March, April, May, and June, and special editions of *Creator* and *Self Portrait* editions. Red Penguin Books has published her pieces in *'Tis the Season's*, *The Flower Shop on the Corner*, and *The Ocean Waves*. Clarendon House Publications published her poems in their *Poetica 2* and *Poetica 3* anthologies, and her work was also included in Ink Gladiator's Press anthologies of *The Rise and Fall of Chimera's* and *Gray, We Hide our Colors Within*. Indie Blu(e) Publishing just published a mental health piece in *Through the Looking Glass: Reflecting on Madness and Chaos Within*, and their newest anthology, *But You Don't Look Sick: The Real Life Adventures of Fibro Bitches, Lupus Warriors, and Other Superheroes Battling Invisible Illness*. 300 South Media Group has published her in *As Darkness Falls* and features her first flash fiction piece in *Sunset Rain*. Train River Poetry has published her in *Poetry 7*. She also appears in *Who's Who of Emerging Writers* by Sweetycat Press. Most recently, she has been published by *Harness Magazine* in their November issue, and in Silent Spark Press *Amazing Poetry*. Brandy can be found online: on Instagram and Facebook @wherebeautifullives, @wherebeautifulloves, or her web page www.wherebeautifulinks.com

Brandy Lane

Brandy Lane

I used to take these quiet times to speak to God.
But nothing happened to my prayers,
unless no answer—is the answer.

So I took that time and turned my prayers into poetry.
Every free moment I had, I would write to a friend.
He used to answer every prompt—
was excited to hear from me.

This year, not so much.

I watched him slowly drift away,
watched him board another ship,
saw him move on.

He's nearly faded from view now.

It really is a different type of grief
when the living act like they're dead to you.

So I went back to praying today.

Wanna know what I prayed for?

For every success and joy to come to him.
For abundant love and validation.
I prayed for him to be happy,
even if it is without me.

Because even though he's not mine,
I will always love him.
I will always want him to be happy.

That is what love is.

♡ B1

Brandy Lane

There is no love here
anymore.

Just images of a beautiful past
of a love that didn't last.

On his end.

Over here?

She's not handling it well.

♡ BL

No Love Here

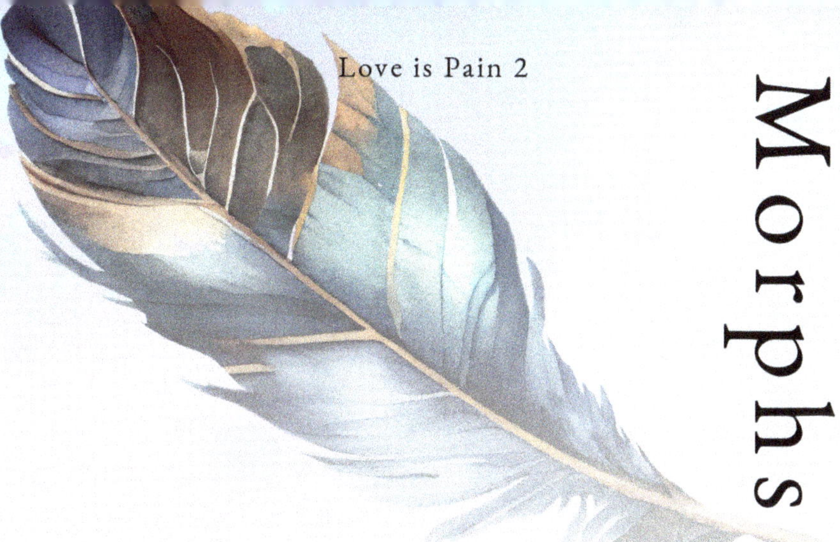

Morphs

As one day morphs into another,
slumber my only respite,
I dream through a haze of memories
and realize I'm feeling desperate.
For what? You ponder, inquisitively
as I stare off into space—
like a neurodivergent lost in a world
unable to match its pace.

For the comfort of family,
the laughter of friends,
for sitting around a table—
For all I had, but now lack,
my past is now mere fable.
Lesson learned: to appreciate
all that we've been gifted,
and in fondly remembering
may our spirits now be lifted.

♡ BL

Brandy Lane

Tell me you don't love me
and I will leave you be.
No more texts, no more notes
no more poetry.

I will try to forget you,
and go about my way
and hope that it'll get easier
day, after wretched day.

I'll push down my emotions
way down deep inside
and pretend that it was just a dream,
when you were by my side.

I thought that we had something
and that it would always last,
but I guess that I was wrong,
because now it's in the past.

But if you DO still love me,
don't say a single word,
because then I'll understand,
though to some, it seems absurd...

but I'll know that even though
you've had to quench that fire...
that somewhere down inside your soul,
I'm still someone you desire.

Desire

My Safe Place

You are my safe place, the one mind I can count on
that my thoughts don't boomerang back toward me—
to crash on walls like thrown objects.

You are a respite to my soul, the only peace in my
chaos, my healer of disdain.

You are my encouragement in a season of lack, the hope
that keeps me going, a place to heal and create.

You are my companion in every weather, every season,
in every beautiful and equally terrifying circumstance.

You calm me.

♡ B1

*I*t wasn't infatuation.
It wasn't an obsession either...

I know this because it has been far too long that I've been away, yet I still think of you every moment I'm awake, and even my dreams are visited by your laughter.

I've tried to move on, but I don't want to forget the most intimate relationship I've ever known... mainly because I don't want it to end.

How do I turn a period into a page turn?

If George Lucas can go back and write prequels and sequels and make the time make more sense as context changes, why can't we?

♡ BL

Prequels

Beauty

$\mathcal{I}$ miss him in the way that missing him is the
hardest thing I've ever had to do.
I have tried to consider what that feeling is.

It's like being on Mars with no green thing... yet,
the eerie orange glow is still beautiful.

It's like being in the desert, yet I can still find
memories of where every grain began...
so there is beauty there as well.

Winter, with its death and naked trees,
and bitter cold...
yet the snow shrouds it all in, once again—
beauty.

What I am feeling is not beautiful,
I feel a void deep within my soul, like a black
hole that sucks all beauty and light
from every living thing.

I'm left with less than nothing.

There is no sound, no light,
no tangible anything at all.

The Divided Realm

That was the night her world was divided into two distinct parts:

The light, where all beauty and love lives, where the mountains reach toward the heavens, and the clouds are made of gossamer sugar strands. The laughter echoes within the hollow realm of her skull because she doesn't want to use her mind for anything but peace.

And the dark, where the screaming and cursing occur, where bruises are hidden on her soul, where no one else can see. The dark waters try to drown her in their cold depths, pretending to be comforting but denying her a place to breathe. Her mind reels, and she begs for an escape from this hell.

She is trapped within these two realms, and the one who she thought was her guide, the one she thought would save her—or at least hold her hand through to safety—has abandoned her. She fears his world is like hers, but he is trapped on the other side, where she can no longer see his plight.

If only she had listened to her heart—if only she had gone down a different path.

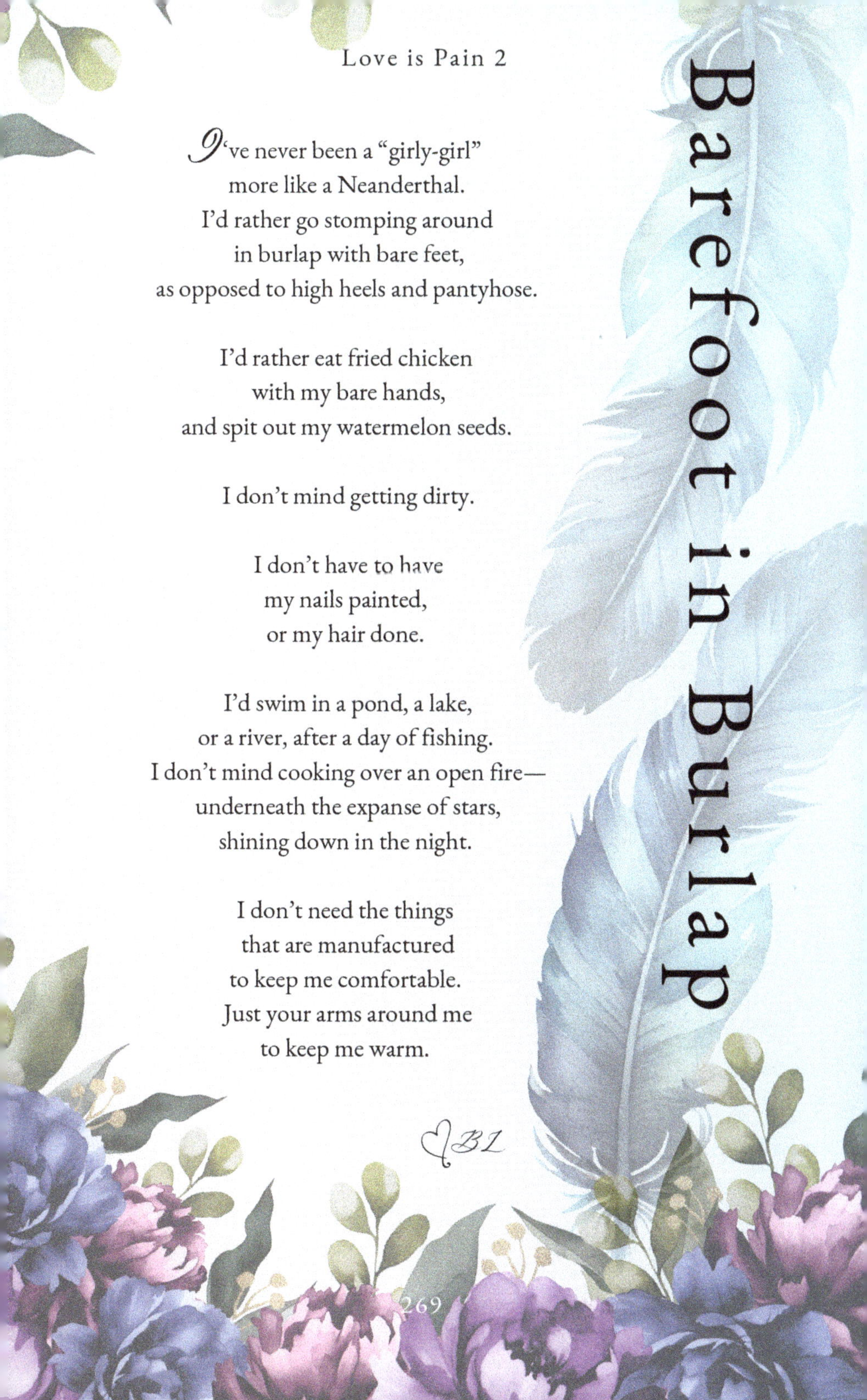

$\mathcal{I}$'ve never been a "girly-girl"
more like a Neanderthal.
I'd rather go stomping around
in burlap with bare feet,
as opposed to high heels and pantyhose.

I'd rather eat fried chicken
with my bare hands,
and spit out my watermelon seeds.

I don't mind getting dirty.

I don't have to have
my nails painted,
or my hair done.

I'd swim in a pond, a lake,
or a river, after a day of fishing.
I don't mind cooking over an open fire—
underneath the expanse of stars,
shining down in the night.

I don't need the things
that are manufactured
to keep me comfortable.
Just your arms around me
to keep me warm.

♡ BL

Brandy Lane

Unbroken

Tell me words
I need to hear
loudly spoken—
the ones
that will keep
my fragile heart,
unbroken.

♡ *BL*

Nothing

Nothing seems right.
Nothing looks right.
Nothing tastes right.
Nothing feels right.
Nothing sounds right.

All because, you left.

♡ BL

Brandy Lane

What would I be;
     without your judgements,
     without your criticism,
     without your jealousy,
     without your condescending looks,
     without your guilt trips,
     without your neediness,
     without your rules,
     without your disappointment,
     without your disapproval,
     without your resentment,
     without your impatience,
     without your disrespect,
     without your mistrust,
     without you lording over me?

What would I be?
I would be free.

♡ BL

I want to want to write to you,
a little poem, or maybe two...
I want to *want* to smile again
to cheer you up and be your friend,
but something has happened to me inside—
something I've been trying to hide.

You see, it's not that I *don't* love you
it's that I don't *want* to want you.

I'm not supposed to feel like this,
like we are in a vast abyss—
where all I feel is awful ache
...and this incredible heartache.

All I *want* to want is you...
but I can't want what isn't true.
I *want* to want so very much;
but I just don't, 'cause when we touch
I want to *not want* to pull away...
but rather want to *want* to stay,

but I can't fix the want to go,
because what I want just isn't so.

♡ BL

I Want to Want

Other books by Brandy Lane:

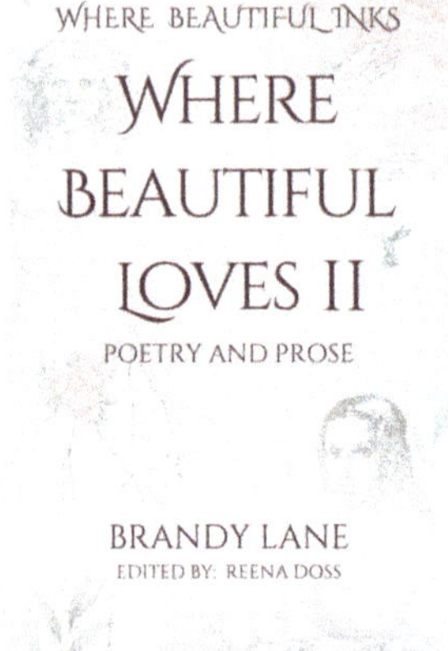

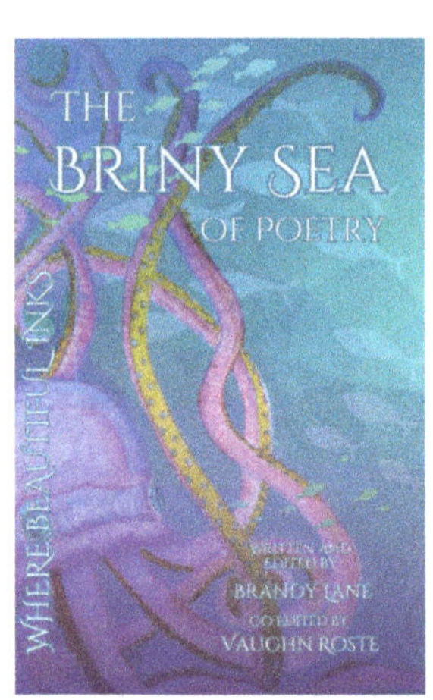

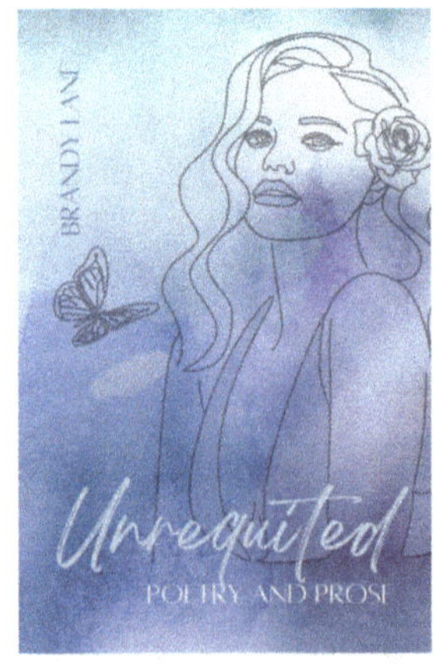

Published by:
Where Beautiful Inks

Anthologies by
Where Beautiful Inks

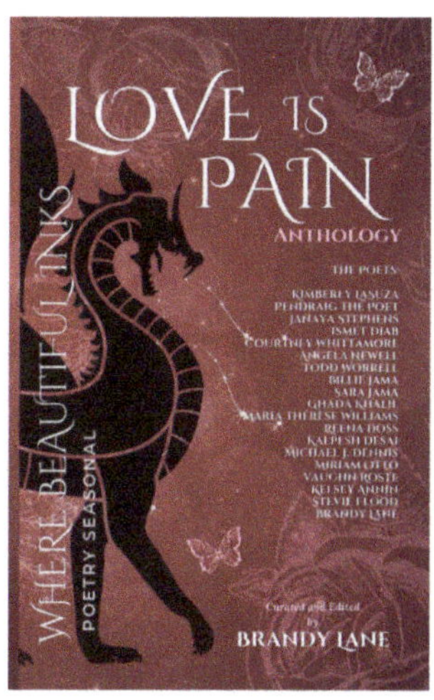

A Guiding Light

These beautiful authors used my services for formatting, cover creation, or publishing consulting.